SUSAN STEWART was a desperate woman. She couldn't bear to lose Dan now. She had committed one reckless act of deceit that would either draw Dan closer to her . . . or push him away forever.

BOB HUGHES was facing the biggest crisis of his medical career—the possibility of dismissal from Memorial Hospital! Before his own eyes, he saw all his precious dreams and ambitions slipping away.

KIM DIXON agonized over the deci... about to make. Two men sai... she couldn't remem... would bring he... would cause her g...

Series Story Editor **Mary Ann Cooper** is America's foremost soap opera expert. She writes the nationally syndicated column *Speaking of Soaps*, is a major contributor to soap opera magazines, and has appeared on numerous radio and television talk shows.

Angelica Aimes, author of *Shared Moments*, is a celebrated romance writer. A native New Englander, she now divides her time between her Manhattan townhouse and her cottage on a secluded island in the Atlantic.

Dear Friend,

Pioneer Communications Network takes great pride in presenting the eighth book in the Soaps & Serials paperback series. If this is your first Soaps & Serials book, you're in for a pleasant surprise. Our books give you a glimpse into the past, featuring some of the most exciting stories in the history of television soaps. For those of you who are old friends of the Soaps & Serials line, thanks for your support.

Here's one of the many questions we've received from our thoughtful and loyal fans. A contented Soaps & Serials reader couldn't remember the name of Penny's sister on AS THE WORLD TURNS and wondered if we could help. Penny Hughes had a sister named Susan but there's good reason not to remember her. She was never seen on the show.

Although we can't answer all the letters we receive, we still enjoy hearing from you. Keep writing!

For Soaps & Serials Books,

Mary Ann Cooper

Mary Ann Cooper

P.S. If you missed previous Soaps & Serials books and can't find them in your local book source, please see the order form inserted in this book.

AS THE
WORLD TURNS

8

Shared
Moments

PIONEER COMMUNICATIONS NETWORK, INC.

Shared Moments

AS THE WORLD TURNS paperback novels are published and distributed by Pioneer Communications Network, Inc.

SOAPS & SERIALS™ is a trademark of Pioneer Communications Network, Inc.

ISBN: 0-916217-48-5

Printed in Canada

10 9 8 7 6 5 4 3 2 1

Shared Moments

Chapter One
Forever Bound

"Happy, sweetheart?" Dan put his arm around Kim's narrow shoulders and drew her closer.

"Mmmm," she murmured, falling easily into step with him. "Happier than I can ever describe."

Listening to the fresh snow crunch beneath their boots, they walked together, so content there was no need to speak. The day was brilliantly clear and as hushed as a church. Each color was brilliant: the blue of the sky, the white of the snow, the black of the stark branches. And up ahead, like two animated dolls, Betsy and Emily kicked a path through the snow, tossing snowballs at each other, their laughter, as pure as the sound of crystal bells, wafting back to Dan and Kim.

"This must have been the way it was at the

beginning of the world," Kim whispered almost reverently. "Before we made a mess out of everything with wars and pollution and all the rest of the garbage."

"It is the beginning of the world," Dan said, smiling tenderly, "at least for us."

"I hope with all my heart it never changes." Kim gazed up at him, her face serious and filled with love.

So much heartbreak and so many broken dreams lay behind them that she was afraid to think too much about their happiness, afraid that it might be lost before they became a true family.

For Kim, loving Dan was a liberation. Although she knew it was unfair, she couldn't help comparing the man she loved, Dr. Daniel Stewart with the man she'd married, Dr. John Dixon. Kim had never doubted John's love but had learned that no matter how she tried, she couldn't love him in return. Instead of freeing her to respond with her whole heart, his devotion had become an iron chain, holding her back. His need was so intense, it was suffocating. Looking at Dan's lean, athletic body, at his dark curls and cleft chin, delighting in the contagious warmth of his smile and the humor reflected in his bright eyes, Kim knew that with him she'd always feel free, like a bird who'd finally been released from a gilded cage.

Dan had lived so long in her dreams, in her most secret fantasies, that even now, seeing him ruddy faced and glowing in the brilliant winter light, she half expected to wake up and find herself in her husband's bed. Kim had been at one of the lowest points in her life when she first met Dan. It had been shortly after the death of her sister, Jennifer, and Kim had finally made up her mind to ask her husband for a divorce. She'd married John Dixon out of desperation—and regretted it ever since.

To her horror, though, Kim found out how much more difficult it was to end a marriage than begin one. John had refused to let her walk out of his life. When every argument he could muster had failed, he ran after her and tried to force her to stay. In his heedless rush, he had fallen and crashed down the stairs.

Kim still remembered looking at the crumpled, broken body at her feet and being overcome by a feeling of the most intense guilt. John's greatest crime had been to love her too much. Once she heard the preliminary diagnosis, she had put the question of a divorce out of her mind. John had been severely injured and possibly paralyzed for life. The doctors had thought he might never walk again. He had married her when she had been in trouble, but in one fateful moment, he had become the one in need. Her guilt had been so great that she had blamed herself for his accident. She could never walk out on the husband she had crippled.

Resigning herself to a life spent caring for

John, Kim had tried to make herself a dutiful wife, conferring frequently with the doctor about her husband's condition. But that had become increasingly difficult because Dr. Daniel Stewart had been working on the case. Little by little, Kim had found herself thinking more about the doctor and less about the patient.

For Dan, too, it had been a dark period. He had been still mourning the sudden, tragic death of his new bride after barely a week of marriage. He had also been trying to be both mother and father to her daughter Betsy, and at the same time convince his first wife, Susan, to give him custody of their baby daughter, Emily.

Neither Kim nor Dan had been emotionally free to admit the growing attraction they had felt for each other, yet at the same time they had been drawn to each other secretly, silently. Unable to handle the tumult of his life, Dan had taken the two girls and moved to England, but some irresistible force had eventually pulled him back to Oakdale.

When he saw Kim again, he had known at once what that mysterious force was. John Dixon had given a cocktail party to welcome Dr. Stewart back to the staff. By then, John had been completely cured. His paralysis had proved temporary. For a while he'd remained in the wheelchair, playing sick to garner Kim's sympathy, but eventually he'd begun to walk perfectly again.

Dan had scarcely noticed his host's cure, though. Instead, his eyes had been fixed on Kim Dixon, and he'd found himself thinking about her the way no man has a right to think of any other man's wife.

Looking back now, it seemed to Kim that she and Dan had waited so long for the happiness they now shared, it made the bond between them even more precious. At first she'd been afraid his daughters wouldn't accept her, but Betsy and Emily had quickly become like the children she had never had. At last the way looked clear for them to have a life together.

Stopping for a moment, Dan smiled into her eyes. "Will you ask John for a divorce?" he murmured as if he had read the emotions that filled her heart. "I want you to be my wife, Kim, the mother of my children, the loving heart of my family."

She answered him with a tender, probing kiss that said more than mere words ever could have. He grasped her tightly and kissed her hungrily. Kim thrilled at the power she possessed to excite this gorgeous man. It was not only his face and body which were so gloriously beautiful, she thought, it was the man himself. He was strong, forthright, sure of his own identity and desires, a dedicated doctor, a devoted father; and she was sure he'd be a wonderful husband.

"I'll have lunch with John tomorrow," Kim promised. "It's just a formality really. I think

11

John has changed. When I left him this time, he didn't even try to stop me or convince me to stay. In fact, I got the odd feeling that he was actually more relieved than anything else. It was finally out in the open. Our marriage was over, not just for me, but for both of us."

Instinctively, Dan hugged her tighter. "I hope and pray you're right, sweetheart, but I wouldn't count on John giving you up too easily."

"Don't worry," she assured him, tucking a stray curl under his ski cap. "I know John a lot better than you do."

"I'm sure you do," he admitted, "but you're so trusting. It's one of the things that makes me love you so. And one of the things that makes me worry about you. I don't want you to be hurt."

"John never meant to hurt me," she answered, feeling it necessary to defend her husband even now because he had been so kind to her once, "even when he was desperate to hold on to me."

"Maybe you're right," Dan conceded. "But even if he doesn't want to hurt you, I'm sure he wants to destroy *us*. You should see the way he looks at me when I meet him in the hospital. If looks could kill. . . ."

Kim laughed away his concern. "Of course, John must feel a little jealous. He's only human after all. But I know he genuinely cares for me, so in his heart he must want me to be happy."

"Do you really believe that?" Dan gazed deep into her eyes, trying to determine if she was sincere or just trying to paint a bright picture for him. Professionally, anyhow, John Dixon was so devious, Dan would never refer a patient to him. It was difficult for him to even imagine that Kim was Dixon's wife. It was more than a waste, it was a travesty, he thought.

Brushing his lips with a tender, teasing kiss, Kim whispered, "Don't worry about John. Letting me leave was the hardest part for him. Granting a divorce now should only be a formality."

Laugh at your fears and they'll disappear, Kim told herself, but no amount of sound advice would quiet the butterflies in her stomach. There was no logical reason to feel as nervous as she did. She was just having lunch with her husband, the person she knew more intimately than anyone else in the world, yet Kim had never felt more tense. So much was riding on their meeting, not only her own future, but Dan's and Betsy's, and little Emily's as well.

John smiled at her across the table and raised his extra-dry martini. He didn't usually drink at lunch, but this was a special occasion. It was the first time he'd seen his wife since she had walked out on him for Dan

Stewart and, if his scheme was successful, the first critical step in luring her back.

"To you, Kim," he toasted, "to your happiness wherever you find it."

Taking a sip of her chablis, Kim met his eyes frankly. She'd never played games with John, and she wasn't about to start now. "That's exactly what I want to talk to you about." For a second, she hesitated. It felt strange to be sitting across the table from her husband in an unfamiliar restaurant as though they were acquaintances instead of a man and woman who had shared the hopes and failures of a life together. Then, mustering her courage, she plunged ahead. "I have found happiness, John, with Dan and his children, and now I want us to be a real family."

John toyed with the stem of his martini glass, his expression betraying no emotion at all. "You're asking me for a divorce to marry Dan Stewart?" His words were as much a statement of fact as a question.

"Yes," Kim answered in a soft, subdued voice. John was so calm, so restrained it was upsetting. She'd expected at least a flash of temper. "I don't want anything from you, John, no alimony, none of the household things, the cars, the furniture," she rushed on. "Only my freedom."

"Then you have it," he said, raising his eyebrow slightly, "but are you sure you can be happy under the circumstances?"

"I don't want to say anything that might

hurt you," she apologized, "but I love Dan very much."

"I'm sure you do," John acknowledged dryly. "But happiness doesn't necessarily follow love. I should know that better than anyone," he added with a short, ironic laugh.

Kim took another sip of her wine and prayed that the waitress would rush their orders. Now that John had agreed to a divorce, she wanted to get away, to end their awkward, vaguely ominous meeting. But he was being so reasonable, so understanding, she knew she shouldn't cut short their lunch. "I'm willing to take that chance," she admitted.

"Are you, Kim?" He gazed at her so long and so intensely that she felt the color rising in her cheeks.

"I'm not sure I understand what you're getting at," she confessed, fidgeting with the corner of her napkin.

"It's simple, really. Do you think you can be happy knowing that you bought your happiness at the cost of Susan Stewart's life?"

"Susan's life?" Kim echoed incredulously. "Don't you think you're being a little overdramatic, John? I know Susan is still in love with Dan, but—"

"Please." He held up his hand to stop her. "Hear me out, first. I'm speaking now, not only as someone who cares very much about you, but as a doctor as well."

Smoothing the edges of the tablecloth with

his fingers as he spoke, John began to spin the web of lies that, he was sure, would keep Kim tied to him—at least legally. As he spoke, Kim was reminded of another meal they'd shared in a restaurant not unlike this one. It seemed like another lifetime ago, yet she remembered every detail.

The week before that long-ago dinner she'd gone to the doctor and confirmed her fears. She was having a baby. In a moment of weakness that they both had regretted, Kim had had an affair with her brother-in-law. Bob Hughes and her sister, Jennifer, had been separated at the time, but were soon reconciled and more deeply in love than ever before. By a terrible twist of fate both sisters had become pregnant in the same month by the same man. Kim had not been able to confess to Jennifer that she was expecting Bob's baby as well.

Kim had been desperate to confide her guilty secret to someone. John had seemed so understanding and sincere that Kim had poured out her heart to him, and by the end of their dinner, he had offered what appeared at the time to be the perfect solution to her dilemma: marriage. A marriage of necessity on her part and of jealous, possessive love on his. Although Kim now believed that marriage was finally behind her, John would never accept that it was over.

"Susan wasn't always an alcoholic," he said. "She began drinking when the court gave Dan custody of Emily. Even though you miscarried your own child, Kim, as a woman I'm sure you can imagine what Susan must have felt when a judge declared that she was unfit to be the mother of her only daughter. Her only mistake was devoting too much time to her career and not enough to her child.

"I have no doubt that Emily suffered emotionally as a result, but Susan has paid an even higher price. First she lost her daughter, then her friends, her job, her livelihood. It's become a vicious circle. The more her losses multiply, the more she drinks."

"She won't listen to Dan," Kim broke in, feeling uncomfortably defensive. "But you're probably her best friend. Why don't you make her go for treatment?"

John shook his head. "No one can force an alcoholic to stop drinking. Susan has to want to help herself. That's the only way the treatment works, and right now she has no motivation." Propping both elbows on the table, he leaned toward Kim and fixed her with a steady, intense gaze. "If you go ahead with your plans to divorce me and marry Dan, it will be just as if you uncorked a bottomless bottle of whiskey and gave it to Susan."

"I can't believe she's as bad as you say, John," Kim insisted. "I know Dan has no idea she's drinking that much. Susan is an intelligent, ambitious woman. How could she do that to herself?"

"Why do we all make terrible mistakes in

our lives?" John answered. "All I can tell you with any certainty is my professional opinion. If you go ahead with your plans to divorce me and marry Dan, I believe that Susan will be dead within a year of alcoholism."

"You can't mean it!" Kim's face turned pale.

Smiling inwardly with secret satisfaction, John only nodded. "Sadly, for all three of you, I do."

"Oh no!" Kim murmured. "I don't know what to do. Susan Stewart has never been one of my favorite people, but I certainly never wished her any harm," she admitted.

Sitting back, John watched Kim wrestle with her conflicting emotions, confident that she wouldn't press him for a divorce now. John knew he hadn't beaten Dan Stewart yet. But as long as Kim was still his wife, there was always a chance that he could win her back.

Chapter Two
Heart to Heart

Dr. John Dixon was sitting at the desk beside the nurses' station when the paging began: "Dr. Hughes. Dr. Robert Hughes, please report to the eleventh floor. Dr. Hughes." Frowning with annoyance, he looked up and saw Bob Hughes hurrying down the hall.

"Who needs Hughes here?" John asked, turning sharply on the head nurse.

"I do," Claire Browning answered pleasantly. "We just transferred one of his cardiac patients from the cardiac care unit to Room 1109. I'd like to get the orders on him before I go off duty."

John automatically checked his watch. It was seven-twenty A.M. His day was just beginning but hers was ending. Claire Browning was one of the best floor nurses at Memorial, and she always worked the midnight-to-eight shift. "Hughes should have called the orders in when the patient was transferred," he said critically.

Claire ignored the comment and went on with her work. It was an open secret at the hospital that no love was lost between Dr. Dixon and Dr. Hughes. Claire was too smart a nurse to get caught between two doctors, yet she couldn't help feeling sorry for Bob Hughes. He had never recovered from his wife's tragic death. Ever since Jennifer had been killed in an auto accident, he'd been inconsolable. It seemed that the only thing he had left to live for was his little daughter Frannie, and, Claire wondered, how could a busy doctor like Bob Hughes care for a little girl alone? The best housekeeper could never make up for a full-time mother, she thought.

"I wish Dr. Hughes would remarry," she said, glancing at John. "It would be good for him—and for his daughter."

"What makes you say that?" John snapped. His conversation with Kim was so painfully fresh in his mind that any mention of marriage made him see red.

"Because he seems so lost since his wife was killed. He must have loved her very much," Claire added.

"Loved Jennifer?" John snorted. "Hughes doesn't even know the meaning of the word. He'll take any woman he can get. Believe me, I know. Look at his track record. He's had three marriages already. His first, to Lisa, lasted long enough to produce Tom. Then there was somebody he picked up on the rebound. Sandy, her name was. I don't think she even stuck it out a year. Finally, Jennifer took pity on him."

"She was your wife's sister, wasn't she?" Claire asked.

"Yes," John replied curtly, and before she had a chance to ask anything more, Bob Hughes came up to the desk, mumbling to himself.

"Oh, Dr. Hughes." Claire smiled brightly. "I'm sorry, I didn't hear what you said."

"Said?" He looked at her blankly for a moment, then he pulled himself out of his fog of depression. "No, I didn't say anything important. I guess I was just talking to myself," he admitted.

"If there's anything I can do, doctor," Claire said compassionately.

"Thanks," he said, forcing a smile. "What you can do is tell me who was paging me."

"That's easy." She laughed. "I was, about Norman Garrison, the cardiac patient you had transferred. He's in Room 1109, but I need orders."

"Of course," Bob said hastily. How could he have forgotten to call in the orders? He was so preoccupied with his own loss that he was forgetting about his patients. Taking the chart that Claire gave him, he wrote carefully, trying to make up for his previous lapse.

As he wrote, though, he became uncomfortably aware of someone watching him. Looking up, he found John Dixon's eyes fixed on him with undisguised loathing. Poor guy, he thought. Bob had always felt sorry for John, but he felt even sorrier for Kim. What could it be like to be married to a man so consumed with jealousy, so insanely possessive?

Kim was a wonderful woman, second only to her sister Jennifer, he thought, swallowing the lump that rose in his throat every time he thought of his dead wife. There had been a time once, a long time ago, when for a few brief days he and Kim had believed they loved each other, but soon they'd discovered they'd mistaken need for something much more lasting. Bob had thought his marriage to Jennifer was finished, and Kim's life had been at loose ends. They'd come together like two lost souls, giving warmth and comfort to each other.

It had been a short-lived affair that they'd both come to regret. Jennifer had understood and forgiven them. But even though their affair had occurred before Kim had met her husband, John Dixon could neither forgive nor forget. Through the years Bob had tried to become friends with John for Kim's and Jennifer's sake. But it was impossible. John couldn't bear to think that another man had slept with his wife. It didn't matter to him that Jennifer was the only woman Bob had ever truly loved. It didn't matter that Bob's affair with Kim had been just a brief moment out of the mainstream of their lives when each had needed someone to cling to. Every time he saw Bob, he pictured Kim in his arms.

"Good morning, John," Bob said, returning the chart to Claire. "Sorry, I didn't see you sitting there before. I've been walking around in a fog, I'm afraid, since . . . since Jennifer," he apologized.

Bob Hughes was a big man, yet he seemed somehow smaller since his wife's death. Although he wasn't as ruggedly good looking as Dan Stewart, and he didn't have the fine features of John Dixon, he had a kind, friendly face that made him appealing.

John stared at him coldly, sure that Bob had heard by now that Kim had left him. Irrationally he blamed Bob for her desertion almost as much as he blamed Dan Stewart. He was going to get his wife back though —one way or another. "I understand you have a cardiac patient on the floor," he began icily.

"Yes," Bob said. "Room 1109. You probably know the man or at least know of him, John. It's such a small world." Bob shook his head. "You remember my second wife, Sandy? We were only married a few months really. Well this guy, Norman Garrison, is Sandy's estranged husband. They're separated, not divorced—at least not yet. When he got into trouble, he called her, and she called me."

A cold fire burned in John Dixon's eyes.

"Some things are never over, are they, Bob?" he asked pointedly.

Listening to the two doctors, Claire Browning shook her head, but she didn't interfere. Like everyone else at Memorial Hospital, she'd heard the gossip: Kim Dixon had left her husband for Dr. Dan Stewart. What woman wouldn't? Claire thought with a twinge of envy. Professionally, though, it made things pretty sticky around the hospital. John Dixon had always been difficult to deal with. Now though, he seemed to have a permanent chip on his shoulder. It was just the opposite with Bob Hughes. Everybody liked him, and in the past weeks when he'd been forgetting orders and making mistakes because he was distraught over his wife's tragic death, the rest of the staff had been trying to cover for him. John Dixon was the only exception. If John caught Bob Hughes breaking hospital rules, Claire was sure that he would be merciless. Even a malpractice suit wouldn't be as damaging as Dixon armed with sufficient ammunition.

"Never over?" Bob echoed John's words, either purposely choosing to misunderstand them or too preoccupied to see their deeper meaning. "My marriage to Sandy was over before it began. I married her on the rebound from Lisa, and she married me because she wanted security. It didn't take us long, though, to realize that we'd both gone into the marriage for the wrong reasons. We never loved each other, but we genuinely liked each other. So we parted amicably, and we've remained friends to this day. That's why she called me."

"Don't you think Garrison minds your taking up with his wife again?" John asked snidely.

"That's what I've just been telling you," Bob said with a sigh, sure that in his present condition, he wasn't making himself clear enough. "Sandy and I are just friends. We have been for years. Even Jennifer accepted that."

"Certainly." A bitter mocking smile turned down the corners of John's thin lips. "Just like you've remained friends with Kim. It's that kind of *friendship* that ruins a marriage."

Bob looked in embarrassment from John to Claire. No matter how hard he tried, it was impossible to have a civil conversation with John Dixon. He didn't know how Kim had put up with the man for so long. She was so fresh, so open, so much like Jennifer in many ways. Bob hoped the rumor was true. If Kim had really left John, he had no one to blame but himself. Bob was sure she would be much happier with Dan Stewart.

Turning away from John, Bob looked at Claire, his eyes speaking the apology he thought it wiser not to put into words. "How is Garrison doing?" he asked. "He practically demanded that I release him from the cardiac care unit and put him in a private room.

Actually I would have preferred to keep him in C.C.U. for a few days more, but he was raising such a fuss that I thought it was wiser to do what he wanted."

"He's not doing badly at all. The figures are all here," she said, looking over the chart with him as if Norman Garrison were the most important patient ever admitted to the Oakdale Memorial Hospital. The conversation between the two doctors was one she wished she had not been forced to listen to. And now that it was over, her relief was so great, she would go to any length to keep them from starting up again.

"We did an electrocardiogram. As you can see, doctor, the heartbeat is still regular." She spoke quickly and intensely, barely pausing for breath so that Dr. Dixon couldn't squeeze a word in edgewise. "The patient's condition remains stable, although he's clearly not off the critical list yet."

"Excellent report, Claire," Bob complimented her, partly because it was true and partly because he sensed her acute embarrassment. "Of course I'll take a look at Garrison now, but on the face of it, I'd say he has a good chance, as long as he remains calm. Any upset at this point, though, could still prove fatal. I'll be sure to warn Sandy—Mrs. Garrison, that is," he corrected himself, never suspecting that the words he spoke would come back to haunt him.

* * *

Norman Garrison lay on his back, his hospital bed raised up to a semi-sitting position, his broad face red with anger. He was a big, burly man, and, although he had been in the hospital for well over a week, he couldn't accustom himself to the idea that he had to remain calm and quiet. The constraints of the I.V. and the monitor checking his heart rate were annoying to a man as active and volatile as he. He wanted desperately to go home. Short of that, he was ready to lash out at everyone who he felt was conspiring to keep him bedridden. He hadn't died. That scare was past, and he no longer had any patience with strict hospital procedures.

Now looking at the doctor standing by his bedside checking his pulse, Norman felt his pent-up frustrations come to a boil. It was bad enough to be sick, but to have your life and your health in the hands of your wife's ex-husband was too much. And to add insult to injury, Sandy treated Bob Hughes much better than she'd ever treated him!

"When am I getting out of here, doc?" he demanded loudly.

Although Norman asked the same question every time he was examined, Bob showed no sign of impatience. "It's too soon to tell," he answered evenly. "But you're progressing nicely. Just try not to let yourself get upset. That's the important part now, and I can't do that for you."

"Oh yes you can, Hughes," he shouted.

"Just seeing you upsets me. I want you off the case. I'm getting myself a new cardiologist."

Bob glanced across the room to Sandy. Until that moment, she'd been pretending to be absorbed in one of the men's magazines that Norman had insisted she buy for him.

Now she slammed the magazine shut. "Norm, what's gotten into you now? You're such a big dumb loudmouth you don't know what you've got here. Bob Hughes is the best in Oakdale."

"Shut up," he thundered. "I don't want to hear how Hughes rates as a lover on a scale of zero to ten . . . I'm your husband now."

"All you can think of is sex. That's the trouble with you," Sandy burst out. "I'm talking about doctors. You can't get anyone better than Bob to take care of you. So unless you want to go out of here feet first, I suggest *you* shut up and do as you're told."

"I'm not listening to any dumb broad. All you know about medicine would fit in an aspirin bottle," he snapped.

"Well, that's a lot more than you know," she countered defiantly. "You're just mad, Norm, because for once in your life, you're the one taking the orders, not giving them."

"Right now, the doctor's orders are to calm down," Bob said firmly, trying to take control of what was clearly becoming a dangerous situation.

Norman began to answer back, but Bob stopped him. "Hold it just a minute and look at the monitor up there." Although his voice was soft, it held an unmistakable note of authority. "You can see exactly what you're doing to your heart. If you keep carrying on like this, you're going to give yourself another heart attack. I won't be able to do much to help you then, Norman," he warned.

"You're not kidding, are you?" The big man's face had paled suddenly and he clutched at his chest as if his heart were already betraying him.

"I've never been more serious in my life," Bob replied. "I want to get you better and out of here as quickly as I can. But I can't do much to help you, if you keep upsetting yourself."

"I'm not upsetting myself," he insisted, the anger rising again. "It's the two of you—you and my wife."

"Former wife," Sandy corrected.

"You're not my ex yet," Norman reminded her, "and you'd better remember it. I may be dumb, but I'm not blind. I know what's going on between the two of you. And I'm not going to lie here and take it."

"Norman, I swear to you," Bob said evenly, "there is absolutely nothing going on—as you put it—between Sandy and me. We were married once a long time ago for a very short time. Since then we've been friends—nothing more."

"I don't believe you . . . either of you," he insisted. "It's not normal. There's no way a man's going to be just friends with a woman that belonged to him."

"Sandy never belonged to me," Bob tried to explain. "She was my wife once—briefly."

"That's right," she piped up, unwilling to be reduced to anyone's possession. "I never belonged to Bob and I never belonged to you either, no matter what you thought."

"You wouldn't dare talk back to me like that," Norman said bitterly, "if that guy weren't here egging you on."

"Listen, Norman," Bob interrupted, "I'm going to leave the two of you now, because the longer I stay here, the more upset you're becoming. No matter what you think, Sandy and I are not having an affair, and we're not going to have one now. I would like the opportunity to help you get better. But if you can't accept that, then I agree with you. You should get another cardiologist to handle your case. When I leave here, I'd like you and Sandy to discuss this calmly and rationally like two adults. Whatever your final decision is, I will abide by it."

"But, Bob—" Sandy tried to break in but he wouldn't let her.

"No, Sandy, the decision has to be Norman's. As long as he feels the way he does, my presence as his physician may be doing more harm than good."

Bob sounded so tired and looked so discouraged, Sandy thought as she watched him leave. She wished there was something she could do to help him. She'd heard the nurses talking among themselves and knew that Bob was depressed over his wife's death. Some small part of Sandy's heart felt the pinch of jealousy. If she died tomorrow, no one would feel her loss so deeply. She'd had two husbands, and neither one had truly loved her. Right now, Norman needed her. But once he was back on his feet again, he'd kiss her goodbye just like he'd done with all his other women.

Norman's snide words cut through her thoughts. At first she couldn't believe her ears, but it was true. Norman was muttering about her and Bob to the resident who'd come in to examine him just after Bob had left. God only knew how many others he'd complained to as well, Sandy thought, her anger growing.

"Get out of here," she snapped at the startled young doctor. "And don't you dare repeat a word of the nonsense my husband has been telling you. It's not his heart that's sick—it's his head," she announced. Although she was a petite woman, Sandy was feisty, and the resident knew better than to get between a jealous husband and an angry wife.

Following him to the door, Sandy closed it with a thud and turned to face her husband, her hands on her small hips, and her chin thrust out belligerently. "Norman!" she nearly shouted, "what are you trying to do? Ruin Bob's reputation and kill yourself in the bargain? I'm telling you once more, and this time I hope it will penetrate your thick skull. I haven't been in bed with Bob Hughes since the day I left him. Is that clear enough for even you to comprehend?" she demanded sarcastically. "And for that matter, even if Bob and I were having an affair, it wouldn't be any of your business. You seem to have forgotten that you and I are separated. We haven't lived as husband and wife for three months. And if I have anything to say about it," she added hotly, "it'll stay that way for the rest of my life."

"You see," he cut in excitedly. "You just said it's none of my business. That proves it—"

"That proves nothing," Sandy snapped, "except that you and I are separated. The reason I left you has nothing to do with Bob Hughes. I've told you a thousand times. Both Bob and I realized very quickly that we should never have married. We got hitched for all the wrong reasons, so we split. There were no hard feelings, no sour grapes. It's as simple as that. I never even asked him for alimony. It didn't seem fair that he should pay me for the rest of his life because we both made a mistake. I don't understand why you can't accept that, Norman, and let Bob get you back on your feet again. You can ask anybody around here, Bob Hughes is the best in Oakdale when it comes to cardiology."

Norman tried to answer her back, but suddenly his breath started to come in short gasps, and he clutched at his chest as if he were in pain again. Sandy read the fear in his face as clearly as if it were printed across his forehead. Watching him, she paled too.

"Hang on, honey," she begged. "I'll go and get somebody to help you."

"No," he gasped, his voice barely audible. "Don't leave me, Sandy. I'm . . . I'm afraid."

"I'll come right back," she promised.

"No!" He forced the word out of his throat, and the anguished cry stopped Sandy. Turning back, she rushed to his side and took his hand, switching the light on to call a nurse just before she did. "Try to breathe evenly, Norm," she urged him. "Take it nice and easy." For all his faults, she still loved her husband. Their marriage had failed because one woman was never enough for Norman Garrison. But Sandy's emotions were still strong. With all her heart, she wanted him to again be the man she'd loved.

"Maybe when Bob gets you better and you're finally out of here, you and I can still work out something together," she promised tentatively. If she kept talking, she thought, the sound of her voice would calm him. It was her fault that Norman was so upset. Knowing the kind of man he was, the kind of macho, jealous husband, she should never have called

Bob, she told herself. But when Norman was having his heart attack, she didn't know who else to turn to.

"It's okay, Mrs. Garrison." A nurse was prying their hands apart and gently leading her out to the corridor. "Your husband will be better now if he gets some rest. The resident will take care of him."

Sandy looked around her like someone in a trance. She hadn't even realized the cardiac team had come in, and now as they started working on Norman, she watched in horror, praying her husband would be all right.

"It came on so suddenly, I didn't know what to do. . . . He—he wouldn't let me leave him," she stammered almost incoherently.

"It's a terrible fright, I know."

"Do you think he'll be all right?" Sandy asked, afraid to hear the answer.

"Of course it's too early to say, but your husband's heart rhythms on the monitor seem to be stabilizing," she said gravely. "I'm sure Dr. Hughes has told you how important it is for a cardiac patient to remain calm. The slightest upset—"

"I know," Sandy broke in, "it could be fatal."

Walking to the solarium to wait until the team of experts finished working on her husband, Sandy stared out the wide windows in the corridor. Outside the day was gray and dismal, just the way she felt. A cold, wet chill forced passersby to huddle into their coats and pull their mufflers tighter around their necks. Would Norman ever make it home again? Sandy wondered. In spite of the nurse's optimistic words, she knew that her husband's volatile temper could well be his death sentence, and again she wondered if calling in Dr. Bob Hughes would prove to be a fatal mistake.

Chapter Three
Hearts Astray

The night was black and long and filled with love. The house was quiet except for the lovers' murmurings as they held each other. Each time they made love, Kim thought, it couldn't possibly be better; and yet the next time, miraculously, it was.

Was that the true miracle of love? she wondered. She began to stroke Dan's back, still warm with the glow of their lovemaking. No matter how tired she was, she would never push him away. At the touch of her hands, though, he turned his back on her.

"What's the trouble, love?" Kim murmured, trying to hide the hurt she felt. "Wasn't it good for you?"

"It was too good, that's the trouble." Dan's voice sounded like a low, angry rumble.

"I don't understand," she whispered.

Turning back, he touched her cheek and felt the moisture of a tear. "Don't you understand?" he murmured, taking her in his arms and cradling her tenderly. "You're wonderful. We're wonderful. But it's not enough. It never can be until you're mine to hold and cherish and love forever."

"But Susan—" Kim began.

"I saw Susan yesterday," Dan said before she could finish. "She came to take Emily shopping and we had a little chat. She's actually quite proud of herself. She's been going to Alcoholics Anonymous for six weeks now, and she hasn't had a drink in all that time."

Kim shook her head sadly. "It's pathetic, isn't it? I suppose that's what she wants you to believe. She's probably afraid you won't let her visit Emily if you know what a hopeless alcoholic she is."

"Kim," he said gently, "I'm trying to tell you, Susan never looked better. I don't think she was lying."

"But John told me—"

"John told you what he wants you to believe," Dan said more sharply than he'd intended. "That isn't necessarily the same as the truth."

Shutting her eyes tightly, Kim tried to sort out the jumble of thoughts that crowded her mind. She didn't doubt for a moment that John would lie to her to get what he wanted. On the other hand, Dan could easily convince himself that Susan was overcoming her drinking problem. He wanted to believe it so much, he might be refusing to face the grim reality.

Which man should she believe? Kim knew that Dan would never deceive her intentionally, but he might be deceiving himself, simply because he loved her so much, wanted her so much. His rich, sensuous voice broke through her thoughts.

"I don't want to go on like this. It's not healthy for the girls, and it's not healthy for me. They can't understand why you won't come and live with us all the time and be their real mother. Now they're beginning to think it's my fault—that I don't want to marry you."

"They can't believe that," Kim insisted. "They must see how much we love each other. Why don't you tell them that we're going to get married as soon as we can?"

"Are we?" Dan asked, turning her face so that she couldn't avoid his eyes.

"Of course we are," she answered as if she couldn't believe he even had to ask such an obvious question. "Marrying you is all I dream of night and day."

"That's all I wanted to hear." Laughing happily, he showered her with kisses. "Let's set a date right now. Betsy and Emily can be flower girls."

Dan stopped abruptly, feeling Kim's body grow tense in his arms. "I'm rushing. . . ."

She nodded bleakly. "I'm sorry, Dan. I'm just afraid. If Susan really is beginning to straighten herself out, think what our marriage now could do to her? It might start her drinking all over again. I don't think I could live with myself—or you—if I had that on my conscience."

Dan inhaled deeply, trying not to allow his frustration to overwhelm him. "You're the most beautiful, unselfish person I've ever known," he admitted. "But it's time you thought of yourself for a change. Don't you see, Kim? You can go on like this for the rest of your life, postponing our marriage because you're worried it might start Susan drinking again. Susan could backslide any time. That's the nature of alcoholism. No one is ever cured of it. So where does that leave us? Are you going to refuse to marry me forever?"

His question rang out in the dim, silent room, and he pressed her closer in his arms, as if he were afraid that she might never be his. His chest felt warm against hers, warm, comforting and strong. Reaching up, Kim brushed his cheek with her fingers. The sharp dark stubble of his beard scratched her hand. She liked a man with a heavy beard, she thought, but then she liked everything about Dan. No, she corrected herself. She loved everything about him. But she had to check her dreams and desires, at least for a while, because Dan was watching her expectantly, waiting for her answer.

What could she say? Kim couldn't refute the logic of his words. She wished their lives were simple. Then she could say what she felt. But their lives *weren't* simple. Kim wanted to do what was best for all of them: for Dan, the girls, Susan, John, and for herself. She couldn't think clearly, though, not when his arms were around her and his lips only inches from her own.

"It's so confusing," she said softly. "Wouldn't it be wonderful if our minds could flash ahead. If we saw what our actions would do, we wouldn't make such a mess of our lives."

"Is that what you think you'd do if you married me?"

Hearing the hurt in his voice, Kim smiled tenderly up at him. "Of course not. Being your wife and a mother to Betsy and Emily would be more wonderful than anything in the world."

"Then why are we wasting our time talking?" Dan grinned like a boy. "What do you say to a February 14 wedding?"

"Valentine's Day?" Kim smiled back.

"Perfect, don't you think? It's the one day in the calendar dedicated to love, and it's far enough away to give you time to make your plans. I know brides don't like to be rushed. What do you say, sweetheart?"

Dan's enthusiasm was so contagious, Kim was tempted to give in. But then John's dire words came back to her: Susan could be dead of alcoholism within the year.

"Can I tell the girls in the morning?" Dan asked. "They'll be so excited. Two flower girls!"

"No . . . not yet . . . please." Kim hesitated. "I just don't know what to say."

"Don't you love me enough, Kim? Is that why you're holding back?" Dan's voice was low and gentle, without a hint of anger or reproach.

"I adore you, Dan," she answered quickly. "You must believe that. It's the price of our happiness that worries me."

"What about the price of our unhappiness if we don't marry?" he demanded. "Have you thought about that?"

Kim shook her head hopelessly. "I can't seem to think of anything clearly when I'm with you—except how much I want you."

"That's good enough for me," he murmured. "Why don't you tell me about that. Or better yet, show me." His free hand swept over her body, driving every thought from her mind except thoughts of love.

In all the years Kim had been married to John, and even during her brief affair with Bob Hughes, she'd never known such consuming desire or such unquenchable eagerness to make love.

"No," she begged, stopping the hand that was stroking her thigh lightly. "That's what the trouble with us is. We can't settle anything as long as we're together."

"What do you suggest?" he asked. "A hands-off policy?"

"I never make any promises I can't keep," Kim laughed, tightening her grip on him. "No, I think maybe I should go away for a few days to someplace where I can be alone to try and think things out, decide what we should do. I made a mess of my life once already. Now that I have a chance to start over, I don't want to make another mess."

Dan's hands stopped cold. He didn't need to be held back any longer. "You mean you want to leave me and Betsy and Emily?" The thought was so crushing, it was painful even to say the words.

"Of course I don't *want* to leave any of you," she said, taking his face in her hands, and bringing it down to her lips with infinite tenderness. "But I need to."

"I can't let you go. Not now, when we've just found each other." Dan's voice caught in his throat and he nuzzled his face against her shoulder, his mouth open against the porcelain coolness of her throat. Although he didn't say anything more, Kim knew he was remembering Liz Talbot.

It had been Liz, a fair English beauty, for whom Dan had first left Susan. It was Liz who was Betsy's real mother. And it was Liz whom Dan had rushed to marry when Susan finally gave him a divorce. When they exchanged their wedding vows, Dan and Liz had believed they were embarking on a long and wonderful life together, but fate had intervened cruelly.

It had been an open secret in Oakdale that Dan Stewart had wanted to marry Liz Talbot even before she became pregnant, but he hadn't been free then, and Susan had stubbornly refused to give him a divorce. Betsy was born illegitimately. And when Susan finally gave in, it was too late for Dan and Liz. Their time together had run out almost before it began. After a small wedding and a perfect week-long honeymoon, Liz had fallen, rushing down the stairs. It had been a fatal accident. For all his skill as a physician, Dan had been able to do nothing to save his new bride. Although he had tried to carry on with his life, the memory of Liz and his failure to save her had haunted him. Finally, Dan had taken Betsy and her half sister Emily and moved to England. Even though he'd met Kim by then, life in Oakdale had been too full of fresh tragedy for him to remain there. And at that point Kim had seemed committed to nursing her husband.

Had Dan loved Liz as much or even more than he loved her? Kim wondered, checking the jealousy that welled up within her. "I'm not thinking of leaving you, Dan," she promised gently. "I just need to go away for a few days to sort out my life. Everything has been happening so quickly. You came home from England and turned my life upside down with a single kiss. Then there was the terrible business with Susan and Emily. And now I'm here with you instead of with John."

"And I've never been happier," Dan broke in, as if he had read the secret jealousy in her heart and understood.

"Do you mean it?"

"More than I've ever meant anything." He smiled, but Kim thought it was a smile tinged with a certain sadness.

"Then show me, love," she murmured, anxious to wipe away any hint of unhappiness or regret.

And he did. Every concern was forgotten as their bodies came together with a sudden, intense urgency born out of need and fear. Their desire was volcanic, flowing hot and thick like lava, scorching their hearts with its intensity. Yet long after, as they lay entwined in each other's arms, the disturbing sense of foreboding lingered on.

The frozen pond beneath her window shimmered like glass. Skaters on silver blades flashed by, leaving fine etchings on the icy surface. Meditatively Kim looked out the window and listened to the bright voices of the skaters calling to each other.

Her heart quickened as she thought how much fun it would be to come back to the lodge with her husband and daughters when she was Mrs. Daniel Stewart. Alone with her own daydreams in the rustic lodge, Kim found herself longing for the family that was almost hers. She'd spent her days away from Oakdale exploring the pond and the neighboring farmland, and her evenings cuddled up in front of the fire that roared in the massive granite fireplace in the game room. But no matter what she did her thoughts were never far from Dan.

Hiking in the bitter cold, she'd wrestled with her conflicting emotions, coming back again and again to the same question: What price would she have to pay for happiness? Could she and Dan build a family on the wreck of Susan Stewart's life? On the other hand, was it fair to deny Betsy and Emily the warmth and security that they needed so desperately and that a complete family could provide them?

Kim smiled thinking of the two little girls. They were her almost-daughters. Long without a mother, Betsy was hungry for a maternal touch, and she'd opened her heart so trustingly and completely that the memory brought tears to Kim's eyes. Emily, though younger, was much warier. It would take time and patience to undo the damage that her mother had done.

Susan Stewart never had any intention of hurting her daughter. The truth was she had no interest in Emily at all. There were only two things that mattered to Susan: Dan and her career as a medical researcher. Emily had simply been a pawn.

Susan had gotten pregnant to keep Dan from leaving her and ending their marriage. When that ploy failed, she lost interest in the baby so completely that Dan took the child with him to England. For the first four years of her life, Emily grew up not knowing her mother. The absence never seemed to bother her. She had a family in her father and her half sister Betsy. When they finally returned to Oakdale, though, Emily's life had changed radically.

Susan had still harbored a secret hope that she could win Dan back, and she had been ready to do anything to make that hope a reality. It quickly became clear, though, that Dan had no intention of letting her back into his life. For him their marriage was permanently over, but Susan had refused to give up. Emily had been the only thing that still tied them together, and so she used the little girl to try to win back her husband.

Confident that no court would deny the rights of a mother whose only child had been stolen from her, Susan went to court to demand custody of her daughter. She had been prepared to be generous in her victory. In fact, she not only offered Dan unlimited visiting rights, she urged him to see Emily every day, but her motives had been far from pure.

Every time Dan saw Emily, he would also see her, and in time, Susan reasoned, his resistance would begin to wear down. But

Susan had miscalculated on several counts. She underestimated the depth of Dan's bitterness toward her for taking his child, and for scarcely considering Emily's feelings at all. Torn from her father's arms and separated from her sister with shocking suddenness, the little girl became withdrawn and frightened. To her, Susan was not a mother. She was a stranger.

Placed in the care of a housekeeper while Susan pursued her own medical career, Emily had grown more and more lonely. She couldn't understand why she was never allowed to go home with her father when he came to visit her, and she couldn't understand why the woman who was supposed to be her mother was continually leaving her.

Finally one evening, unable to bear the sadness that had become her constant companion, Emily ran away to find her father and sister. But the little girl had no idea what direction to take, and the longer she wandered, the more frightened she became. Still she didn't turn back. She never wanted to return to her mother's house.

Hours passed before Susan, in desperation, called Dan. Half of Oakdale joined in the search for the missing child. Teams of police with specially trained dogs tried to pick up her scent, but it was almost morning before Emily had been found, huddled in the back of a deserted panel truck across town. Although she suffered from shock, Emily had been unharmed physically. The emotional scars, however, were more difficult to measure.

Susan hadn't dared to protest when Dan picked up his daughter and carried her home to the house she'd been searching for. Watching him walk away, though, Susan had known that her gamble was over. She not only lost the child she'd never wanted or loved, she lost the man she would love forever.

Once he had Emily back, Dan had lost no time in petitioning to have the court order reversed. He not only won full custody of the little girl, he had Susan declared an unfit mother and her visiting rights severely restricted. This time, Susan didn't try to fight him. Instead, she turned to alcohol for solace.

The high, infectious laugh of one of the skaters on the pond below brought Kim back from her memories. There was no one to blame for what had happened. Susan, Dan and Emily had each in a way been victims, and each had suffered.

The effect on Emily was difficult to measure. Would she ever trust a woman again, Kim wondered—especially a woman who tried to be a mother to her? Maybe with enough time and enough love she would. Kim could only hope. For Susan, though, the emotional devastation was all too apparent.

She was paying for her actions with her own health, Kim thought. Was her guilt so deep that she drank to erase it? Although she had restricted visiting rights, Susan had never once tried to see Emily. Maybe she was afraid her daughter would reject her now.

As Kim mused on all the variables that had brought the Stewarts and Dixons to such a critical juncture in their lives, the excited voices of the skaters died away unnoticed. The night temperature dipped into the teens, and the sky became black and studded with stars.

In the solitude of the winter lodge, Kim had finally made her choice. There was risk in every decision, but she, Dan, Betsy, and Emily deserved a chance at happiness. Dan had been right. They could postpone their wedding forever, and Susan still would not be cured. Alcohol was a problem that she would have to conquer anew every day. Although Kim sympathized deeply with Susan, she had finally come to accept a basic truth: four lives could not be sacrificed in the hope of saving one.

Taking a sheet of paper, she began to write a letter to Dan. Her heart was so full of joy that she wanted to share her emotions with him. Although she would be his third wife, she felt as if they were beginning their life together with a clean slate. The mistakes of the past were wiped clean; the sad memories, the bitter losses were tucked away in a safe corner.

"My dearest Dan," she began, "I have never been filled with such inner peace and utter contentment. It is a vast, starry evening, and I long for your arms around me. Yet I am not lonely, because I know at last that we will be together very soon—and forever.

"Yes, dearest, my mind is clear of doubts finally. A Valentine's Day wedding with two little flower girls will be a dream come true."

Folding the letter carefully, she slid it into an envelope and sealed it. But there was no point in addressing or mailing it. Now that her decision was made, she couldn't wait to get back to Oakdale and personally give Dan the letter.

Chapter Four
An Untimely Death

Bob Hughes looked up at the starless sky and shivered in the chill night as he approached Memorial. It was an inhospitable evening, cold and pitch black, the kind of night to curl up in front of a blazing fire with a mug of cocoa and a good book. Bob had made his rounds in the morning, visiting each of his patients. There was no need for him to check on them again. Yet neither had there been anything to keep him home. Frannie was sleeping soundly. The housekeeper had gone to bed hours before. The big house had felt lonely without Jennifer, and he'd been concerned about Norman Garrison. Garrison was so unpredictable, Bob thought as he entered the hospital. He would sleep more soundly knowing his patient was resting calmly.

Hanging up his overcoat in the doctors'

lounge, he put his stethoscope around his neck and took the back elevator to the eleventh floor. The bright hall lights were dimmed for the night, casting the long narrow corridor in shadows. There was really no reason for him to be there, he thought. Loneliness, not a medical emergency, had driven him out into the cold night, loneliness for Jennifer.

Thoughts of his lost wife filled his mind. If it weren't for his little daughter Frannie, he wouldn't even try to go on living without her.

Preoccupied with his own dark thoughts, Bob didn't notice the person hurrying along the corridor, until the shadowy figure brushed past him. By then it was too late to see who it was or even to determine if it was a man or a woman. All Bob noticed was the figure's face was hidden behind a big fur collar. Probably a visitor who stayed behind long after visiting hours were over, he told himself. Every now and then some friend or relative escaped the nurses' routine check.

Bob immediately forgot the encounter, though, when he reached Norman Garrison's room. With a light knock he pushed open the door and tiptoed in. If Garrison was sleeping, he'd just check the monitors, he thought. But three steps into the room, Bob realized something was terribly wrong. Garrison's body was flung across the bed, as if he'd tried to get up, then fallen backward. The monitors that were supposed to record his heart rate were eerily still.

"Damn," he muttered, rushing to the bedside. With quick, expert motions, he checked the pulse, then putting on his stethoscope, listened for a heartbeat, knowing as he did that he would hear nothing. Poor Sandy, he thought, reaching for the buzzer to summon help.

But before he could switch it on, a young resident burst into the room followed quickly by Claire Browning. Bob recognized the younger man. Peter Marin was one of the brightest, most ambitious residents at Oakdale Memorial.

"How did you get here so fast?" Bob asked grimly. "I was just about to call you. Garrison is dead. He must have suffered another attack and tried to get up to get help."

"To get help or get away from you, Dr. Hughes?" The resident was eyeing him strangely, distrustfully.

"What do you mean get away from me?" Bob demanded. "I just walked in here and found my patient—"

"You *just* walked in, Doctor?" Marin challenged. "We could hear Garrison down the hall. He was angry and shouting. Obviously he was having a fight with someone."

Bob frowned in disbelief. "But there was no one here when I came in," he started to explain.

"Precisely," the resident said sharply.

"Are you accusing me of causing my own patient's death?" Bob was so dumbfounded he could barely ask the question.

"I'm not accusing you of anything," Marin replied. "I don't have to. The facts speak for themselves."

"Claire?" Bob turned beseechingly to the nurse who stood pale and shaken, listening to the bitter exchange.

But instead of defending him, she shook her head as if she couldn't believe the evidence before her. "Dr. Hughes, you said yourself, any upset could be fatal."

"True enough," Bob conceded. "But what could have upset him? We weren't arguing. I just walked in myself and found him like this. There was no one else here." For some strange reason, Bob felt the need to defend himself in front of Claire. Peter Marin would walk over his own mother to get where he wanted to go, but Claire Browning was a different story. She was one of the finest nurses at Oakdale Memorial.

"I heard the voices distinctly all the way down the hall," Marin insisted. "It had to be Garrison. Garrison and—"

"I'm not going to stand here arguing with you," Bob cut in abruptly.

Peter Marin met his eyes with a cold, steely glare. "I'm going to get the patient on a respirator and call in the emergency cardiac team," he announced.

"What the devil for? I told you Garrison is dead." Bob snapped.

"Under the circumstances, doctor, I don't think we should trust your word alone," Marin answered defiantly.

"Okay, call in whomever you want. But you're just wasting your time," Bob insisted. "I've been a doctor for twenty years, and I know a dead man when I see one."

Taking off his stethoscope and angrily jamming it in his pocket, he brushed past the resident.

Peter Marin reminded him of a young John Dixon. He'd only been at Memorial a few months and already he had earned a reputation as a very smart young doctor and an enormously ambitious one. No step was too ruthless if it brought him closer to his goal. Although Bob could understand that kind of single-minded drive, he could never condone it.

As he walked away, he could hear Marin issuing orders as if he were the chief cardiologist. Bob shook his head sadly. Marin could use every extraordinary means of resuscitating Norman Garrison in the book and it wouldn't change the outcome. Garrison was beyond help.

Pausing at the nurse's station, he telephoned Sandy. The next of kin had to be notified, and he wanted to break the news himself. Sandy was a friend as well as his ex-wife. She had entrusted her husband to his care. In spite of Marin's accusation, Bob knew he wasn't responsible for Garrison's death, and he wanted to assure Sandy of that before she heard the malicious gossip that was sure to spread all through the hospital. In many ways Memorial Hospital was like a small town. It was impossible to keep a secret.

When he heard Sandy's voice, still groggy with sleep, Bob explained what had happened simply and concisely. He knew there was no easy way to break the news of a loved one's death. Memories of the phone call that told him of Jennifer's accident flooded over him. It had been so unexpected, so shocking, he was still trying to adjust to the terrible reality, still trying to deal with the feeling of total devastation that had swept over him. Now, hearing Sandy's voice break, he felt her grief almost as strongly as his own.

Although she and Norman were separated, Sandy had loved him to the end. In many ways he had been a difficult man, short-tempered, volatile, jealous, unfaithful. But he had also been warm and generous, and she would mourn his loss deeply.

Hanging up the phone, Sandy went back to bed, but sleep was impossible. She stared at the ceiling and thought of the strange turn her life had taken. An urgent need had brought her two husbands together, yet from the first Norman couldn't accept Bob, couldn't bear the thought that his life was in the hands of Sandy's former lover. In the most secret recess of her heart, Sandy had been glad that he'd been jealous. Now she felt nothing but regret.

What had upset Norman enough to trigger a fatal attack? she wondered. Although she'd played on his jealousy of Bob, even relished it, Sandy never imagined that it could kill her husband. Even now, she couldn't believe it. For all his loud, angry talk, Norman knew that her relationship with Bob had been over years before. He'd only accused her of unfaithfulness to ease his own guilty conscience. The truth was just the opposite. She'd never cheated on him, and he'd never been faithful to her, not since the beginning of their marriage. He didn't know the meaning of the word.

Norman usually denied that he had had other women on the side, even when he'd stayed out all night and come home the next morning reeking of cheap perfume. Now he was gone—not for a night but forever. Instead of relief, she felt a deep, gnawing loss. Had he been frightened when he died? Or did the end come so quickly he didn't realize what was happening? Sandy wished she'd been with her husband during his last moments, but Bob had said he'd been alone. That, at least, brought her some consolation. At least he hadn't died in his girlfriend's arms. Tina Richards had been an open secret in their lives. In fact, Sandy had seen her going into the hospital several times. She'd always rushed by as Sandy was leaving—a coarse-looking woman with the collar of her fur coat pulled up around her painted face.

Overnight, Bob Hughes felt as if he'd become a leper. For years he'd walked through the corridors of Oakdale Memorial Hospital confident of his reputation as a good and honest physician. He'd enjoyed the respect of his patients and colleagues. Now, suddenly, he felt like a marked man—a murderer. Orderlies, nurses, even other doctors went out of their way to avoid him or so it seemed to him.

Bob knew that he'd become overly sensitive since the night he found Norman Garrison lying dead, and people like John Dixon only fed his paranoia. John never missed an opportunity to make a snide, biting comment about Bob's reliability. Others on the staff, though more sympathetic, were nonetheless convinced that Bob was in some way responsible for Garrison's death. Whispering among themselves, they came to the unshakable conclusion that Bob's depression since Jennifer's death had affected the way he cared for his patients.

Whenever Bob went into the doctors' lounge now, he felt like a pariah. There were still a few doctors—staunch, loyal friends like Dan Stewart—who stood by him and urged him to fight back. But they were the minority. The news had spread quickly through Oakdale Memorial. Rumors of a huge malpractice suit against the hospital caused the board of directors to act swiftly. In spite of his long, dedicated service, Bob was called on the carpet by the hospital administrator for his handling of the Norman Garrison case. Although he wasn't suspended, a full investigation was called for, which would culminate in a board hearing. He, more than anyone, should know better than to argue with a cardiac patient, the administrator warned.

Although Bob tried to look at his situation optimistically, the handwriting on the wall seemed painfully clear. If he was found guilty at the hearing, he could be suspended or even dismissed from the hospital. The resident's account of the evening was damning, and Bob had nothing but his own word to stand on. There was no one to corroborate his story.

Worse than that, it seemed as if just about everyone at the hospital had already decided he was guilty of malpractice at the very least, if not manslaughter. It was easy to believe that he and Sandy were having an affair. He was lonely without Jennifer, and she was unhappy over the breakup of her marriage. It was easy to believe that Norman Garrison was jealous, he'd been such a volatile man. And certainly he'd been angry the night he died. Claire Browning was sure she'd heard him. At least that gave Bob some comfort. Whatever he thought of Peter Marin's word, he knew Claire would tell the truth.

None of the pieces seemed to fit together. Norman Garrison had been alone when Bob found him. Would even a hot-tempered man like Garrison be shouting at the walls so loudly, so furiously that he gave himself a massive coronary?

Bob was too despondent even to try to find the answer. For years Memorial Hospital had been an integral part of his life. Now, increasingly, he began to dread every moment he spent there. When he walked into the record room, it had seemed crowded. But the moment he sat down, it emptied. With a surge of bitterness, Bob realized he had never known how many fair-weather friends he had. Ironically, he'd come to prefer John Dixon's open hostility. Unfair though it was, at least it was consistent.

Bundling up his stack of unfinished records, Bob stuck them under his arm and started out. He'd finish the paperwork at home where at least he didn't feel as though a scarlet letter were branded on his forehead. Forcing himself to look straight ahead to avoid any embarrassing meetings, Bob made a beeline for the front door. He was crossing the driveway to go to the doctors' parking lot, when a white Lincoln pulled up beside him.

"Bob, are you all right?" the driver called.

The sound of a concerned voice came as

such a shock that he stopped abruptly. Sandy Garrison was leaning out the window, her pretty face creased with worry.

"Okay, I guess." Bob managed a small smile. "I'm very sorry about Norman."

"Not nearly as sorry as I am about what Norman's death is doing to you." Sandy shook her head as though she still couldn't believe the ironic turn of events.

"It's not your fault, Sandy." Bob started for his car again.

"Wait a minute—please. I want to talk to you, Bob, if you can spare the time."

He laughed bitterly. "It looks like pretty soon I'll have all the time in the world."

"What do you mean?" she asked anxiously.

He shrugged. He'd gone beyond the point where anything in his life mattered except Frannie. "Haven't you heard? The hospital is probably going to suspend or dismiss me."

"After all these years? They can't do it!"

"They can," he said emotionlessly, "and they most likely will. They don't want to be slapped with a million-dollar malpractice suit."

"Malpractice suit?" Sandy couldn't believe what she was hearing. "There's only one person who could sue for malpractice over Norman's death and that's me. Do you honestly think I'd do that to you, Bob?"

"Now that you put it that way," he admitted sheepishly, "I guess I don't. I've been so upset over the whole business . . . coming right after Jennifer . . . I haven't been able to think clearly."

Gritting her teeth with steely determination, Sandy leaned across the carseat and pushed the door on the passenger side open. "Get in, Dr. Hughes," she ordered imperially. "You and I have a lot of talking to do, but I don't think we should do it right here in the hospital parking lot. Too many prying eyes."

Bob sank into the plush seat and sighed deeply. Ironically, he and Sandy were much better friends than they'd ever been lovers. Looking at her now, he saw the determination beneath her pretty, almost doll-like features. Sandy's life had not been easy. But the hard knocks had strengthened her.

"Where are we going?" he asked as they pulled onto the main road.

"Who knows?" She shrugged. "I'm dying for a cup of coffee, but I don't think we should be seen together—at least not until this mess blows over. We don't have anything to hide, but you know how things can be misinterpreted. All it takes is one malicious tongue, and our talk will be turned into a lovers' tryst and spread all over Oakdale."

Bob nodded. Much as he hated the whole dirty business, Sandy was right.

"That's why I ambushed you in the parking lot just now," she said.

"Is that what you call stopping an old friend to say hello?" Bob managed his first laugh in weeks.

"I've been waiting for you for hours," she admitted, "hoping you'd come out because I was afraid to go to your office. We need to talk about Norman's death."

"First of all," Bob said, touching her arm in a gesture that spoke more sympathy than any words could have, "I'm truly sorry. I think you loved Norman more than you like to admit."

"I did." She swallowed hard. "And the funny thing is I think he loved me too. That's why he was so jealous of you. But we just couldn't live together. Or maybe it was being married that ruined our relationship. Norman was the kind of guy who wanted every woman except his wife. We were happy together until he put the ring on my finger."

"I'm sorry, Sandy," Bob said again. In his practice he'd heard many women tell the same story. Patients poured out their hearts to him as if he were a confessor, not just a physician. It was a matter of confidence he knew. Like a priest, a doctor was bound to keep his patient's secrets to himself.

"Not half as sorry as I am." Sandy laughed harshly. "But that's so much water under the bridge, and now you're the important one. I feel so guilty, Bob," she admitted, glancing at him, her eyes brimming with tears.

"You? What do you have to be guilty about?" he asked.

"Everything!" Sandy blurted remorsefully. "I blame myself for this whole ugly business. I should never have called you when Norm had his first heart attack. If I hadn't taken advantage of our friendship, you wouldn't be in trouble today."

"That's ridiculous," Bob assured her, although every word she'd said was true. "Your husband got sick, and you called the only doctor you knew. It's as simple as that."

"I wish it were," Sandy murmured, although it was a very painful admission to make. "But to be absolutely truthful, I think when I called you, a small part of me wanted to make Norman jealous. You see, our marriage had just broken up, and I was pretty sure he had another woman."

For a moment Bob didn't utter a word. He simply stared straight ahead at the black line of road that stretched in front of them. "You didn't tell Norman that we were having an affair, did you, Sandy?" he finally asked.

"No, no, of course not," she answered, then smiled ruefully. "I didn't have to. Norm always thought the worst of everyone."

Bob forced himself to remain calm, knowing how difficult the confession must be for Sandy. But he was so tense, he felt that he might snap at any moment. "When Norman accused us, I trust you denied it," he said tightly.

"Yes." Sandy's voice became an embarrassed whisper. "But you know how it is. Sometimes if you deny something indignantly enough, the denial has a false ring to it."

Bob inhaled deeply. "Why are you telling me all this now, Sandy?" he demanded.

"Because I feel so guilty . . . as if I used you, and now you're paying for it with your reputation, your career, everything."

"You didn't cause Norman's fatal heart attack," Bob reminded her, but his voice sounded hollow.

Looking at him now, so dispirited, so despairing, Sandy could barely recognize the earnest young doctor she'd once exchanged wedding vows with. It seemed so many lifetimes ago. It was almost as if they'd been different people then, yet deep down, underneath the layers of pain and loss and experience, she knew they were the same.

"I've got to do something for you, Bob," she insisted. "I feel so responsible. I just can't sit by and watch your whole career destroyed."

"It's not your fault," he told her, sounding tired. "How can I make you believe that?"

"I'm going to have Norm's lawyer write a letter to the hospital," she said firmly, brushing aside his question. "I'll swear that I have absolutely no intention of bringing a malpractice suit against anyone. That should get you off the hook."

"It's a nice try, Sandy," he said despondently. "But the fat is already in the fire. I know hospitals. Once the directors have gone this far, they can't back down no matter what you swear. They'll be relieved that you won't make them pay up, but they won't cancel the hearing."

Sandy looked at him, wishing he were wrong, yet knowing in her heart that he wasn't. His career was on the line. No matter what he said, she couldn't get over the feeling that it was her fault. Norman had lived his life shouting. It was inevitable that he would die the same way—with or without Bob Hughes. But how was she going to convince a medical board of that?

She squeezed his hand. "I'm just not going to let them get you, Bob. I don't know what I'll do, but believe me, I'll think of something," she promised.

Chapter Five
Storm Warnings

Kim looked around the deserted bus station, thinking how much busier Oakdale was, even at seven o'clock in the morning. There wasn't a single person in the waiting area. Hoisting her shoulder bag higher, she walked to the ticket window, conscious of the loud click her heels made.

"When is the next bus to Oakdale, please?" she asked, checking her purse for the tenth time that morning to make sure her return ticket was tucked into the zippered compartment.

"Today?" The clerk stared at her, his round face filled with surprise.

"Yes, this morning," she assured him. "The sooner the better."

"Haven't you heard the news, lady? Tornado warnings are in effect today and tomorrow."

Kim smiled serenely. Nothing could annoy her today. She'd gone to bed at four in the morning and woken up two hours later, brimming with energy and excitement. The world had never looked brighter. Now that her decision was made, she felt as if a cement block had been lifted from her heart and been replaced by an infinite wealth of love. "Actually, I haven't read a paper or listened to a radio in a week," she admitted. "But I guess the world has gotten along well along enough without my notice."

Reaching under the counter, the clerk pulled out a local newspaper and handed it to her. "You'd better take a look at this, then maybe you'll change your plans. The next bus to Oakdale moves out at 8:07 A.M.—that's if it's running today," he warned. "Weather around here can be pretty tricky, you know. One minute it looks perfectly clear, then before you know it, a tornado is whirling into town, sweeping up everything that gets in its way."

"It must be terribly frightening," Kim said.

The clerk was shaking his head ominously. "You can't believe how bad it is until you've seen one of them. You and me, we could be standing right here, and one of those storms could come barreling down the street out there, ripping up everything—houses, cars, kids, cows, trees—and the folks just a block away wouldn't feel a thing except maybe some sand and dust."

Kim greeted the man's dismay with a glowing smile. "I'm sure you're absolutely right," she admitted readily, "but I'll let you in on a little secret. I feel so wonderfully happy today, I must be on the side of the angels. I'm going home on your 8:07 bus to Oakdale to marry the dearest man in the world, and I don't think anything could harm me today, even your terrible tornadoes."

"I wish you luck, lady," the clerk muttered, still shaking his head. "But don't say I didn't tell you."

Kim took the paper he'd given her and checked the clock. She had almost an hour to wait. Although she wasn't the least bit hungry for anything except the irresistible taste of Dan's kisses, she crossed the street and went into a coffee shop to kill time. Sitting down in a vacant booth by the front window, she ordered coffee and a doughnut and started to read the local paper.

The weather was the biggest story on the front page, and Kim opened the paper to a full page of photographs showing the devastation caused by previous tornadoes. No wonder the ticket clerk was afraid, she thought, as she began to read. Living in an area where the weather could turn lethal any moment must make everyone feel skittish. Life in Oakdale was so much more predictable. Soon her mind drifted back to the new home she was returning to and her new life as Mrs. Daniel Stewart. She felt young and starry-eyed again.

Dreams do come true, Kim thought. They were happening to her and to Dan, and she would make them happen for Betsy and—

The waitress's scream cut short her reverie. Her order banged on the table, coffee splattering in every direction. "It's coming right down Main Street!"

Trying to clean up the mess with paper napkins, Kim followed the terrified girl's gaze and gasped. The scene outside the window was worse than a horror movie. Half the street was still sunny and bright. But the other side—where the diner was located —was shrouded in deep shadows. In the distance, headed directly toward them at an unbelievable speed, was a giant black spiral.

"We've got to get out of here!" Kim yelled.

Grabbing the terrified waitress by the arm, she ran for the door. But the manager was already there, holding back his panic-stricken customers. Kim recognized some of the faces from the lodge, only now they were distorted by fear.

"No way we'd ever make it if any of us step out this door," the manager warned. "The tornado's coming at us too fast." He slipped the bolt in the lock as he spoke, making them prisoners. "Our only chance is to get down to the cellar—all of us—and pray." His voice was sharp. He was doing the thinking for all of them, and he expected to be obeyed.

Herding the small cluster of petrified customers and staff in front of him, he directed them through the kitchen to the cellar door. Kim fought back her own fear. Sobered by the manager's commanding manner, she tried to calm the others, murmuring assuring words. In fact, she was so occupied trying to buoy the others' courage that she was about to start down the cellar steps before she remembered that her precious letter to Dan was in her pocketbook. In her panic to escape the tornado, she'd left it in the booth where she'd been sitting.

Ignoring the manager's warning, she rushed back. It was just a few steps, she told herself, and the letter would mean so much to Dan, even more than words because he could keep it always.

Grabbing her bag from the red plastic seat, she looked up. The window was in front of her, black as night. Kim tried to scream, but no sound came.

Moments before the giant spiral had looked as if it was a mile in the distance. Suddenly it was here, on top of her, a lethal, inescapable monster. Before she could move, the plate-glass windows shattered. The walls collapsed like playing cards, and she was being picked up like a rag doll, still clinging to her purse, thrown up, swallowed, lost in the angry, churning vortex of the storm.

In seconds, the coffee shop, which had stood for forty years, was a pile of glass shards and wood splinters, and Kim's dreams were hurled away on the devastating winds.

"Dan! Dan! I love you," she thought she screamed. But she couldn't remember.

Switching on the TV for the evening news, John Dixon put his feet up on the coffee table and reached for the bologna sandwich he'd fixed himself for dinner. Bologna with mustard on rye was hard to take for the third time in three days, but he'd gotten tired of eating out alone. It depressed him.

"One hundred-fifty miles northeast of Oakdale a killer tornado has cut a path of death and destruction through two states," the anchorman was reporting in a portentous voice.

"Let's hear something good for a change," John muttered to the set as he bit into his sandwich. He wasn't interested in coming home after spending the day with sickness and death, only to be faced with violent-storm warnings and reports of vicious crimes on the nightly news.

The picture had switched from the blandly handsome face of the anchorman to the scene of the tornado. "Accident crews are still sorting through the rubble that this morning was a picturesque little lakeshore village," a breathless local reporter said. "At this time it is impossible to say how many lie dead or injured in the wake of this storm. Rescue operations are expected to continue through the week, and with each day the number of victims will surely mount."

The report was still going on when the phone rang. Lowering the volume on the television, John swore under his breath and went to answer it. It never failed. Every time he sat down to relax, a patient called.

"John Dixon speaking," he said mechanically. But a second later his voice sharpened. "Yes, Kim Dixon is my wife."

His face turned a sickening gray; and gripping the table for support, he stared in horror at the silent screen. "There must be some mistake," he began. "Kim—my wife is right here in Oakdale. At least, I think . . . You what? All her identification cards were found in her pocket. That's how you traced me."

John sat down heavily and gripped the receiver tightly to keep his hands from shaking. He'd ignored the storm warnings in his marriage, and lost his wife. Now somehow, Kim had been caught again in a very different kind of storm, and he hadn't even bothered to listen to the news report. If he'd been looking closely, he might have seen Kim—*his* Kim —lying there, an unclaimed body.

"Yes, yes," he answered hollowly. "I'll be able to identify her. She's my wife."

The stark hospital room was transformed into a greenhouse. Floral arrangements banked each wall, thickening the air with their sweet scent. Flowers were admitted but by doctor's orders, no visitors were.

Kim's eyelids fluttered, then opened, and she inhaled deeply, breathing in the rich perfume. She glanced around the room, looking at each flower while she murmured its name softly. It was so strange, she thought with discouragement. She could remember the names of flowers but not the faces of the friends who had sent them. There was so much she couldn't remember. So many thoughts and memories seemed to lie buried in the back of her mind. She kept reaching and reaching for them, but just when it seemed as if she could grasp them, they slipped away again.

"Kim Dixon, Mrs. John Dixon," she said thoughtfully, then repeated her age, address, and telephone number for the umpteenth time, hoping that they would open the locked door of her mind.

Her first memory was waking up in the hospital room of the Oakdale Memorial Hospital the day before with John sitting anxiously at her bedside. She'd recognized him immediately. But she couldn't remember anything about their life together or why she was in the hospital.

"I was in a freak accident," she reminded herself, repeating the words that John had told her. "I went to visit friends and was caught in a tornado. I'm lucky to be alive."

Lucky to be alive! With no past to define

her, no bonds of emotion to tie her, Kim didn't know what being alive meant anymore. Dozens of people had been killed in the tornado but she had escaped with minor cuts and bruises—and a severe memory loss.

Amnesia! It was something that only happened in movies, Kim thought. Yet here she was lying in a hospital bed, feeling utterly lost and trying to piece together the fragments she could remember of her life. Faces looked familiar, names sounded a bell in her brain, but she had no idea who were her friends, and she had no memories of her own feelings. It was almost worse, she told herself, than remembering nothing. A face would float into her mind and she would see something in it like a distant glimmer of light yet no matter how she tried, she couldn't remember.

"How do you feel this morning, Kim?" John came in without knocking. "You've been sleeping for twelve hours," he added as he leaned down and kissed her lips.

"It didn't help at all," Kim said, wondering why the touch of his lips didn't excite her. Was that, too, because of the amnesia? "It's so frustrating," she admitted. "You know what it feels like when you're trying to remember a name? It's right on the tip of your tongue, but you can't seem to say it. Well, that's the way I feel. Except I'm not trying to remember a name, I'm trying to remember my whole life."

John took her hand. "You've got to give yourself time," he assured her. "You suffered a severe blow to the head in the tornado. Everything is still up here," he said stroking her forehead. "You just can't find it yet. How many times have you put something away so safely, you can't remember where you've hidden it? Well, that's more or less the way it is with your memory. Don't try too hard to remember," he added warningly. "If you do, you might impede your recovery."

"What can I do, then?" she asked hopelessly. "I don't even know who I am—if I have family . . . friends."

John reached down and kissed her lips again. "Let me remember for both of us, Kim," he said with a satisfied smile. "Then you won't strain yourself."

Smiling back at him, Kim touched his cheek in thanks. "You're so good to me, John, and I feel like such a useless burden."

"You could never be a burden, darling, not to me," he assured her. "I just thank God that I got you back."

"That's what you think now. But what if my memory never comes back . . ." Her voice broke.

"I told you not to worry. Let me do the remembering for both of us," John repeated. "Soon we'll both be happier than we've ever been before."

Although Kim nodded in agreement, there was something in her husband's voice, something in his expression, that made her wary. There was something John wasn't telling her, but what could it be? Was she brain damaged? Was her memory lost forever?

Long after John had left to make his morning rounds, Kim lay in bed thinking. She'd never felt lonelier in her life or more frightened. Even the bathrobe that John had brought her from home didn't look familiar, she thought as she slipped it on and walked to the window. At first when she stood up, she felt lightheaded, but in a few seconds the sensation passed. At least I don't have to be bedridden, she thought gratefully, as she pulled up the venetian blinds.

Kim peered through the window hoping to spot some familiar landmark. But the morning was bleak. A light drizzle was falling from a gray, overcast sky, and the view below was nothing but an expanse of parking lot. Figures hurried from their cars to the hospital entrance, but they were too far away to recognize.

Discouraged, Kim turned away. She might as well go back to sleep. It was better than this terrible frustration of not being able to remember. The pale green hospital walls seemed to stare back at her, as bare as her own mind. There were so many questions she wanted to ask John, but she was afraid to reveal the utter blankness of her mind, her heart.

As she sank back into the pillows, she heard a light knock, then the door opened. "Good morning, Mrs. Dixon. How do you feel today?" A nurse came in armed with an electronic thermometer.

For an instant Kim stared at the girl, then a smile broke through her gloom. "I remember you—Margot," she said reading the name on the nurse's pin.

"Sure you do," the girl said brightly. "I was in yesterday morning, same time, to take your temp. Let's see what it is today."

Without giving Kim a chance to say anything more, Margot stuck the thermometer under her tongue and took her wrist to check her pulse.

"Everything's normal," Margot said. "That should cheer you up, Mrs. Dixon."

Kim shook her head bleakly. "It probably should, but it doesn't," she admitted. "I know I'm lucky to be alive. My husband says a dozen people were killed in the tornado. It was the worst in a hundred years. But I feel so miserable . . . so, so unattached, like a little boat lost in a vast sea. That probably sounds silly to you," she laughed self-consciously.

"Not at all." Margot sat down at the edge of the bed and squeezed Kim's hand reassuringly. "Amnesia must be the strangest feeling. I mean not knowing where you've been or what you've done. But it's got a positive side too. In a way you're luckier than the rest of us, because you can start all over again with a clean slate. You have no guilt, no regrets, no mistakes to live with for the rest of your life."

"I never thought of it that way," Kim admitted.

"That's not all," Margot went on, encouraged. "You've got so much going for you, Mrs. Dixon. You have wonderful friends, who care about you and want to do everything they can to help."

"I do?" Kim looked uncertain.

"Sure you do," the nurse assured her.

"That's strange." Kim frowned. "Not a single soul has been in to see me since I got here except my husband."

"Of course not." Margot laughed. "Don't you know? You're not allowed visitors or phone calls."

"Why not? I'm not really sick. At least amnesia isn't contagious."

Margot shrugged. "You'll have to ask your husband that. Maybe he wants to keep you quiet. But I can't begin to tell you how many people have called the floor inquiring for you. And then there are the doctors."

"What doctors?" Kim broke in curiously.

"Well, there's your brother-in-law, Dr. Hughes," Margot began.

"Bob Hughes," Kim said, excited that she recognized the name, "and my sister, Jenny —his wife, Jennifer. Why hasn't she come to see me? Surely John—"

The anguished expression on the nurse's face stopped her. "Why? What's the matter, Margot?" she asked quickly.

"I'm sorry, Mrs. Dixon. I guess you don't

remember. Your sister was killed in a car accident. Dr. Hughes is a widower now."

Leaning back, Kim shut her eyes, but the expected burst of grief didn't come. Although she had not remembered that Jenny was dead, deep in her heart she had known it. Her loss was permanent, but her grief was over.

"Dr. Hughes comes by every day to see how you're doing," Margot was saying, trying to fill the void.

"Next time, ask him to come in," Kim said opening her dry eyes again. "I'd like to talk to him. Maybe it would help me jog my memory, at least about my family."

But Margot shook her head. "You'll have to talk to your husband about that. He's left strict orders that no one is allowed in this room, not even other doctors on the staff."

"I don't understand it," Kim admitted. "My husband knows how lonely I feel. I'd love to have some company, even for just a minute or two."

Margot blushed, uncomfortable with the turn the conversation had taken. Although she was new at Oakdale Memorial, she'd heard the other nurses talking. If what they said was right, Dr. Dixon was afraid to let his wife have visitors. Afraid she would remember too much. There was one man in particular he feared, another doctor, but Margot wasn't sure which one.

"Who else has been asking for me?" Kim inquired. She was as hungry for information as a beggar for a crust of bread. Margot didn't have the heart to refuse her.

"Well, Dr. Stewart comes by at least once a day to see how you're doing. Dr. Dan Stewart?" she repeated when Kim showed no sign of recognition.

"Dan. Dan." Unaccountably, just the sound of the name made her feel warmer, safer, as if the sun had broken through on a stormy day. Kim couldn't remember his face, and yet there was something buried deep in her mind, in her heart, struggling to be free. "Dr. Dan Stewart," she repeated the name slowly. "He must be a friend, a very good friend. I'll have to ask my husband about him," she murmured. "What does he look like?"

Margot blushed a deeper pink. "Just between you and me," she said with a giggle, "he's absolutely gorgeous and a widower, too. Rugged, broad-shouldered with dark curly hair and a deep cleft in his chin. There isn't a nurse at Memorial who wouldn't take off with him if he snapped his fingers."

"That's strange," Kim said, lost in her own confused thoughts. "I keep having a dream about a man with dark curly hair. That's all I can remember about him, but he's at the end of a long street. There are children with him—two girls, I think—and they're all calling to me. I begin to run toward them. I run and I run and I run, but I always wake up before I reach them. It's so strange . . . and sad. When I wake up I have the feeling that I've lost something very precious, but I don't know what."

"Maybe it's the children," Margot suggested, touched by Kim's anguish.

"John and I don't have children. I already asked him about that," Kim said.

Margot simply shook her head.

"Then who can the girls in my dream be?" Kim went on. "They *are* girls. I'm sure of that now." She would have to remember to ask John. He would know better than anyone.

Chapter Six
So Near and Yet So Far

Kim sat in the one armchair in her hospital room. A packed overnight bag was at her side. She was dressed in a flowered challis shirtwaist that John had said belonged to her. Looking at herself in the mirror, she thought the print looked vaguely familiar. And it fit well enough, considering the fact that she must have lost weight during her time in the hospital. The room was stripped bare of the few things that had given it a vaguely personal feeling.

Kim was going home—wherever that was. She knew the address, but she couldn't remember what the house looked like inside or out. John had assured her that once she saw it and looked at the furniture, the bric-a-brac, the pictures on the walls, it would seem familiar. But Kim waited nervously, wondering if her husband was right. He was going home with her, but he'd been delayed. One of his patients had been rushed into the emergency room. It seemed she'd heard him being paged hours before, but waiting felt more familiar to her than anything else. She must have gotten used to it being a doctor's wife, she thought.

Remembering so little, Kim grasped at the slightest straws to try and rebuild the life that had been wiped from her mind. Yet even as she did, a warning voice within her sounded like a buoy bell in a stormy sea. Be careful, it seemed to say. She had the opportunity thousands of people only dreamed of: to start her life all over again with a clean slate. Maybe she shouldn't try to remember. Maybe she should start a new calendar for herself, and this would be day one A.D.—after the disaster. And yet she felt rootless, disconnected. Even her face seemed to belong to a stranger. Was she generous or mean-spirited? Loving or cold? Courageous or frightened?

Going to the mirror, Kim studied her reflection closely. She knew what kind of person she would like to be, but what kind of person was she? The face staring back at her with anxious, gentle eyes was one she liked. She wasn't beautiful, certainly, by any classic standard, but she was attractive. She must have loved deeply, and suffered as well, in her forgotten life. It showed in the cast of her eyes, the set of her mouth, the thrust of her chin. Hers was not the bland face of a passionless woman, she was relieved to see.

Kim was still assessing her mirror image critically when the heavy door seemed to open slightly. At first she thought it was her imagination playing new tricks with her. But as she watched through the mirror, she saw the door move again another crack.

"John," she called tentatively. "Is that you?"

At her words, the door opened wider, then closed quickly, shutting Dan Stewart in the hospital room with her. "Kim! Kim!" he kept repeating in a reverent whisper. "It really is you, and you're safe, unharmed. I've been so worried, but John wouldn't let me near you. He's kept you locked away from everyone who cares about you."

All the while he was speaking, Kim was staring at his image in the mirror, wide-eyed and tense. "Who are you?" she managed to whisper.

Dan had started to come toward her as if he intended to take her in his arms, but her words stopped him cold. "You couldn't forget, Kim." He blurted out the words in shock. "Not us. Not what we had—no, what we *have*—together. There's no amnesia in the world that could wipe our love out of your heart," he insisted. Even though he was a doctor, even though he knew how absurd his words were, they were spoken, not by a physician, but by a man and a lover.

Kim turned slowly from the mirror and faced him. Unaccountably, she felt a strange tingling sensation begin to spread through her body. He was six-feet tall or so, and undeniably handsome. He had tender, concerned eyes, a crown of dark curls, and lips that curled up in a hopeful smile above a deeply cleft chin. She knew he was a doctor from the white coat he was wearing over tan gabardine slacks and a striped shirt. Dr. Dan Stewart.

Kim spoke the name aloud, and a smile broke through the deep concern that was etched on his face.

"You *do* remember!" he almost shouted in joy.

But even as he spoke, her head was shaking, back and forth, denying him hope. "I recognized you because one of the nurses described you to me. You're quite a popular guy around Oakdale Memorial from what I hear," she added smiling.

"Are you sure that's why you recognize me and not because . . ." The light went out of his eyes as she continued to shake her head.

"I'm sorry," she murmured. "Were you a friend?" Kim forced her voice to remain even, forced herself to remain standing just in front of the mirrored bureau, forced herself to resist a strange, undeniable power that seemed to draw her closer to him. The more she stared at him, the more familiar he seemed. It wasn't so much the way he looked as a feeling that seemed to unite them, leaping across the chasm of lost memory that divided her from the rest of the world.

"You might call me a friend," he said slowly. "But I could think of a thousand words I'd rather hear you use."

A nervous laugh escaped from her dry lips. What had she been to Dan Stewart? What kind of a woman was she, unfaithful, promiscuous? Her eyes widened with horror at the thought, yet she couldn't honestly rule out any possibility. "You must be a friend of my husband's, then?" she said doubtfully.

"A friend of John Dixon!" Dan laughed harshly. "I think it would be more accurate to say John Dixon hates my guts. That's why he's been keeping you locked up here like a prisoner. He wanted to make sure that I couldn't see you."

"No!" Kim stopped him. "I won't listen to that kind of talk against my husband," she said loyally. "I don't know what I would have done without him. He's been absolutely wonderful to me, helping me fill in the huge blank that's supposed to be my life."

"Please, Kim, try to understand," Dan pleaded. "John has been keeping you isolated from everyone who loves you so that he can invent the life he wants you to remember. The truth is far different from anything he'll admit to you."

"I don't understand," she broke in. "Was I such a terrible person?"

"Terrible?" he echoed in disbelief. "You're terrific."

"Then what would he want to keep from me?" she asked, feeling somehow that Dan Stewart was a man she could trust.

"Us, for one thing." Dan inched closer to her as if she were a deer who might leap away, alarmed by any sudden motion. "I don't want to lay too much on you all at once, but John is trying to kidnap your mind—and your heart."

"I'm not sure I want to hear any more," she broke in nervously. "I'm afraid I won't like the person I am."

"You're the most wonderful person in the world, Kim. Ask my daughters, Emily and Betsy, if you don't believe me. You remember them, don't you?" Kim seemed to brighten at the mention of the girls, and the subtle change didn't escape Dan's intense eyes. "They can't understand why you don't come home to them."

"Home?" Kim echoed the word in confusion. "John is taking me home today."

"No," Dan insisted gently. "He isn't taking you home. He's taking you to his house—the house you left, the life you left."

"But John is my husband," she murmured, trying desperately to sort out the wealth of conflicts that was suddenly being thrust into the emptiness of her mind.

"He was your husband, Kim, but you left him. I don't want to shock you with too much all at once, but I have to tell you this because I don't know when I'll get another chance to see you. John is determined to keep you isolated until he's brainwashed you into believing that you and he were a happy, loving couple. The truth is the exact opposite. Kim . . ." Dan yearned to take her in his powerful arms and hold her and tell her all there was to tell, but he didn't dare to do it. He knew he had to be patient, to give her time to remember, time to open her heart and mind again. But he knew, too, that he had to plant at least the seeds of truth in the fertile soil of her mind before John closed it to everything except his own twisted dream. "Kim," he repeated with utmost gentleness, "before you lost your memory, you had asked John for a divorce, and I had every reason to hope that you would marry me. In fact, the reason you were at the lake when the tornado struck was to decide on your answer."

"But—" she started to speak.

"No." Dan moved close enough to take her hand. "I don't expect you to accept it all right now, but I want you to think about it. Think of everything I've told you as seeds of memory to work with and nurture. With time, Kim, and luck and patience, they will grow and you'll remember." Reaching for her hand, he took it in both of his and brought it to his lips like a precious treasure. "When you do remember, no matter how long it takes, I'll be waiting to reclaim our love."

The pressure of his lips, full and soft and

moist, against her fingertips caused a shudder of delight to course through her. Kim closed her eyes, secretly wishing that he would kiss her yet feeling shamefully guilty of the desire. She was a married woman, and this man, causing her heart to pound so rapidly, was not her husband. In fact, if the nurses were to be believed, he was the heartthrob of Oakdale Memorial Hospital. And yet . . . and yet . . .

Try as she did, Kim couldn't make herself mistrust him. There was some undeniable bond between them that drew her irresistibly. Until he'd walked into her room, she'd had no one to believe except John. He seemed so tender, so concerned, so patient. Yet if Dan's words were true . . . Kim shook her head, as if she could toss away the confusion.

I am Mrs. John Dixon, she told herself. But if that was the whole truth, then why did her husband's kisses turn her lips to stone and the brush of Dan Stewart's mouth against her skin cause her to tremble with desire? He was more than a stranger, more than a friend. She felt it deep in her heart. But was he her lover? Kim felt her cheeks burn at the thought. She wasn't that kind of woman . . . or was she?

Looking up, Kim found his eyes holding her as closely as any man's arms ever could.

"Why did you come here today?" she asked, almost accusingly.

"I've been trying to see you from the moment I discovered you'd been brought here. I was frantic with worry when I learned about the tornado. But your door has been barred by an unyielding jailer."

"You mean my husband?"

"Your ex-husband," he corrected, "in everything except the law. I love you, Kim, and you love me. That's why I'm here, begging you not to close your mind and heart to the promise of that love."

"But I'm a married woman," she repeated as if it were all she had left to hold on to.

"Every marriage wasn't made in heaven," he reminded her gently. "Some, like yours, were a matter of expediency, desperation. You shouldn't feel guilty because you made a mistake. You've paid for it a thousand times over."

How had she paid and for what? There were a million questions Kim wanted to ask, yet she was afraid to. Her life had no parameters, no direction. She was like a blind person, feeling her way through unknown terrain fraught with danger. "You'd better go now," she said, her soft voice filled with apprehension, "before John gets back."

For a long moment, Dan continued to hold her with his eyes. Then he nodded, reluctantly. "If you want me to, Kim, I'll go. But for God's sake, remember," he begged. "Please, remember."

Kim stood motionless, rooted to the exact spot where he left her, until the door closed behind him. Then slowly, like someone in a dream, she turned back and studied her reflection in the mirror again.

Which man do I love? she wondered: John, her concerned, very protective husband or the magnetic, exciting man who had just entered her life with gale force?

The disturbing question kept returning in the days and weeks that followed, even though John kept a virtual lock on Kim's thoughts. Skillfully he contrived to plant selective memories in her mind so that she would remember the ideal life he envisioned for them and nothing else. He was playing God, creating Kim's memories as if her mind were putty for him to mold. He never left her alone. When he was working, a nurse was always on hand. Although John insisted that Kim wasn't well enough yet to be left alone, that her memory was so fragile she might wander off and forget where she lived and how to get home, the nurse was actually there to guard her from her old friends and especially from Dan Stewart.

Dan waited and waited for Kim to remember their love. It still burned so intensely in his heart that he couldn't believe she had truly forgotten it. But she never called, she never came to him. When he went to her house, the nurse turned him away at the door, insisting that Mrs. Dixon wasn't home. And when he telephoned, the same woman always answered and told him that Kim wouldn't speak to him and didn't want him to call again.

At first Dan was sure it was a diabolical plot of John Dixon's to keep Kim away from him and away from everyone who could help her remember the truth. But gradually, his faith began to waver. Emily and Betsy couldn't understand why Kim never visited them anymore. They missed her almost as much as he did, and he had run out of stories to explain her continued absence. Amnesia meant nothing to a lonesome child crying in bed at night for the mother that had almost been hers.

If he had been alone, without his two little daughters constantly begging him to bring Kim back, Dan might have been able to hold on to the slim thread of hope that bound him to her. But the girls' sadness hurt him so much that he made a promise to himself. He would wait for Kim until Valentine's Day, the day he had proposed for their wedding. If that special day didn't rekindle her lost memory, then he would have to accept her amnesia as irreversible. But how could he go on living in Oakdale, knowing that the woman he loved without reservation was just blocks away, yet an eternity away from his arms? How could he live with the knowledge that John Dixon had recaptured her love?

Even though he had weeks to resolve his dilemma, the date rushed up on Dan too soon. There were pink and red hearts in every store window reminding him of the approaching day. But there was no word from Kim, no sign that there was any point in continuing to hope against hope. Without that sign, without some assurance that she would one day come back to him, there was nothing for Dan in Oakdale, nothing except heartbreaking memories.

Kim saw the hearts, too, but she was never allowed to browse in the shops and read the Valentine's Day cards that might have sparked some long-buried memory. Whenever she went out with John or her nurse and tried to stop, she was always hurried along with one excuse or another. It was the same way when the doorbell or the telephone rang. It was always somebody trying to sell her something. She'd been given the same answer so many times that she'd stopped asking who it was.

Since she came home from the hospital, Kim had lived a completely isolated existence. At first she'd tried to rediscover friends, to put some shape and meaning to her life, to solve the puzzle that she'd been trying to piece together in the hospital; but gradually she had given up. Under the guise of helping her, John had succeeded in thwarting her so thoroughly that she'd almost stopped wondering about what had been. Putting aside the questions that seemed impossible to answer, Kim began to believe that John's way was best. She should begin a new life and stop worrying about what was or might have been.

Although he realized it was futile to hope, Dan was counting the days, and finally the hours, until Valentine's Day. Kim had to remember. Even if her memory had failed, her heart could not betray them so cruelly. But even as February 14 came, and Dan waited hour after empty hour, John Dixon was making absolutely sure that Kim would remain his and his alone.

Inhaling the rich perfume of the long-stemmed red roses he'd brought her, Kim smiled across the table that John had set just for the two of them. The flickering candlelight softened the sharp, cynical lines of his face, as he leaned closer and reached across the table to take her hand.

"Do you remember what Valentine's Day is all about, darling?" he murmured as he brought her fingers to his lips and kissed them.

"I think so." She nodded somewhat tentatively.

"It's the one day in the year set apart to show how much we love each other."

She felt his grip tighten around her fingers and suppressed the shudder of apprehension that had begun at his words. "I know that," she admitted. "But there's something else about Valentine's Day, something even more special. It's right there, nagging at the back of my mind, but just when I think I'm about to remember, I lose it again. You must know, John. What can it be? Something just between us, maybe?" Her voice rang with hope, but her face wore the same strained, anxious expression she'd had for weeks.

John shook his head. He always seemed to be shaking his head when she needed an answer, Kim thought with frustration.

"No, darling," he assured her. "There's nothing else for you to remember so don't torment yourself needlessly."

For once Kim refused to be sidetracked. "I'm sure there is something—something too special to forget," she insisted.

"What could be more special than loving you?" His eyes dancing with desire, John stood up and pulled her into his arms. "Tonight I want to show you how much I love you."

Instinctively, she tensed at his embrace. Then, feeling guilty, she slipped her arms around his neck. John had been so good to her since the accident, and so patient. He was her husband and she loved him, Kim told herself. Yet if that was true, why did she recoil from his touch? Why did his kiss turn her to ice?

He was kissing the lobe of her ear and whispering against it, his voice low and tense with anticipation. "I don't want to rush you, darling, but it's been so long, and I love you

Soaps & Serials™ Fans!

★ Order the *Soaps & Serials*™ books you have missed in this series.

★ Collect other *Soaps & Serials*™ series from their very beginnings.

★ Give *Soaps & Serials*™ series as gifts to other fans.

...see other side for ordering information

You can now order previous titles of *Soaps & Serials*™ Books by mail!

Just complete the order form, detach, and send together with your check or money order payable to:

Soaps & Serials™
120 Brighton Road, Box 5201
Clifton, NJ 07015-5201

Please <u>circle</u> the book #'s you wish to order:

The Young and The Restless	1	2	3	4	5	6	7	8
Days of Our Lives	1	2	3	4	5	6	7	8
Guiding Light	1	2	3	4	5	6	7	8
Another World	1	2	3	4	5	6	7	8
As The World Turns	1	2	3	4	5	6	7	8
Dallas™	1	2	3	4	5	6	7	8
Knots Landing™	1	2	3	4	5	6	7	8
Capitol™	1	2	3	4	NOT AVAILABLE			

Each book is $2.50 ($3.50 in Canada).

Total number of books
circled _____ × price above = $ _____

Sales tax (CT and NY residents only) $ _____

Shipping and Handling $ _____ .95

Total payment enclosed $ _____
(check or money orders only)

Name _____

Address _____ Apt# _____

City _____

State _____ Zip _____

Telephone (_____) _____
Area code

ATWT 8

so much. I want to show you what we had together, what we'll have again. Please, darling," he urged, his arms tightening around her, pulling her against his body.

Kim felt the strength of his desire and shuddered. Why did her husband's touch fill her with fear? Why did her thoughts leap back to the doctor in the hospital with the dark curls whenever John held her? Dr. Dan Stewart was just a womanizer, the Don Juan of Oakdale Memorial. Every nurse in the hospital mooned over him, she told herself. And yet . . .

Mistaking her shudder of apprehension for one of desire, John kissed her ardently. Kim began to struggle, her nails raking down the length of his back in her frenzy to escape. Then she checked herself, forcing herself to submit. What right did she have to deny her husband, especially on Valentine's Day?

When he put his arm around her and started up the stairs to the master bedroom, Kim didn't protest. No matter how much she dreaded what lay ahead, she would submit. It was the least she could do to repay her husband. He deserved a wife in more than name only, she kept telling herself.

John's eyes gleamed with satisfaction as he and Kim entered the bedroom that they hadn't shared since the day she walked out of his life. Now he was going to reclaim her, and this time she would be his forever. She would never again possess the freedom, the courage, the independence to leave him. He would make absolutely sure of that. He would keep her tentative, unsure, confused about everyone and everything except that she was his wife. Valentine's Day would be the first day of the new life he had planned for them.

Chapter Seven
Too Late for Love

It was Valentine's Day and Dan Stewart sat alone in his study watching the hands on the brass clock above the fireplace move slowly, steadily toward midnight. Betsy and Emily were sleeping upstairs, oblivious to the momentous decision forming in his mind, a decision that would change their lives completely. There were only fifteen minutes left for Kim to call, and if she didn't there would be nothing to keep Dan in Oakdale any longer. The clock finally struck midnight, and Dan knew Kim was lost. Their love had been wiped out forever by a cruel twist of fate.

Now he realized how fickle, how capricious life was. Luck had run out for Kim and him, he thought, as the day ended in ominous silence. There was no recourse for him now except to run out too, to take the girls and go as far away as he could. He had to find someplace new, someplace where it would be easier to forget, where there would be no memories, no ghosts of love to haunt him.

Once his mind was set, Dan acted swiftly to end his empty life in Oakdale. First, he wrote a letter of resignation to the hospital, next he instructed his secretary to notify all his patients, then he went to the travel agency and bought three one-way tickets to Montevideo, Uruguay, because it was the farthest spot he could think of at the moment. Finally, he sat down with Betsy and Emily to tell them his plan. Although they were too young to understand, Dan still felt he owed them an explanation.

He tried to concentrate on the future and not think of Kim or of what might have been. But she had a way of insinuating herself into his thoughts, even when he wanted, more than anything, to escape from her and from the futile waiting for her memory—and her love—to return. There was certainly enough to keep his mind occupied with preparations for the move. The sooner they left, the less time the girls would have to brood about the big change in their lives, he thought, and so he booked the first flight he could get, one that left forty-eight hours later. Between packing for the three of them, outfitting both girls for the trip, and settling his business affairs, there wasn't a second to spare. There wasn't even time left to say good-bye to his friends.

It's better that way, he thought bleakly. There had been so many farewells in his life, so many abrupt, unexpected endings, that he preferred just to close the door and go as far away as possible.

He wouldn't mind being relieved, at least for a while, of the pressures of life and death that he dealt with every day. He felt deeply responsible for the well being of each of his patients, and when he failed, he always blamed himself.

At least, far from Oakdale where every object, every blade of grass seemed marked with a memory of Kim, he could try to start again for the girls' sake. Emily and Betsy would learn a second language in South America and discover a new culture. *It will be a wonderful learning experience for them,* he told himself, *better than any school.*

But even in his own mind, the words had a hollow ring. The girls loved Kim as completely as if she were their true mother. How could they be happy anywhere in the world without her?

The morning was almost over. The sky was a brilliant blue dotted with snow-white clouds. The sun had already climbed high, rousing the laziest sleepers. Still Kim lay in bed, wide awake, her eyes tightly shut. She'd awakened hours ago, long before the alarm had sounded, long before John had stealthily gotten up trying his best not to wake her. Opening her eyes very slightly, she'd watched him dress and tiptoe out of the room. Instead of getting up then, she'd shut her eyes again to lock out the memory of the night before.

It seemed so innocent when she thought about it unemotionally. It was only natural for a husband to make love to his wife, but the force of the encounter, the intensity of John's response had had a strange effect on her. Something had been wrong from the very first moment he'd touched her. At first the feeling had been undefined, but gradually, the memories had begun coming back, seeping slowly through her consciousness like sunlight filtering through a thick bank of clouds. As her memory trickled back, her mind began to fill again; and, as it did, the undefined sensation crystallized. It wasn't the act she had performed that felt wrong, it was the partner.

Lying in bed beside her husband, making sure that she was so still he assumed she was sleeping, Kim had pried her locked mind open little by little. As she did, the confusion cleared and the life she'd lost took shape again. Through the haze of memories, through the cloud of vague shadows, one face, one name, one special person had shone as clearly as the sun: Dan! Kim repeated the name to herself as if it was a prayer.

He'd tried to tell her in the hospital, but she'd been too frightened, too uncertain, too confused to understand. Besides, she'd trusted John, believed him, depended on him. Now though, she lay in bed, shutting out everything except the memories that grew clearer and clearer. It was like a fog rising, she thought in awe. Yet she was afraid to move, afraid even to open her eyes for fear of losing the fragile thread linking her once more to the life—and the love—that she'd lost in the tornado.

Dan! Dan! Kim formed his name with her lips, and a picture of him took shape in her mind as perfectly as a photograph. The glorious memory of their love flooded over her, warming her heart more powerfully than the whitest heat. But even as she glowed with the warmth of that memory, a fear was rising in her heart. What if she was too late? What if her memory had been restored too late to salvage their love?

The nurses' words came back to her: "A hunk! The best catch at Oakdale Memorial." Remembering their gossip, Kim was afraid. Had Dan already replaced her in his heart? How could she expect him to resist when her amnesia seemed so hopeless and so many other women were lined up, waiting to comfort him? If only she had mailed her letter to him instead of deciding to give it to him personally. Now the letter and so much more were lost.

Kim opened her eyes in the dim room and looked around her. The curtains were still drawn, denying the day and the hour, which was almost noon. The room, the furnishings, the knickknacks that she had so recently rediscovered now felt like a stranger's. John had come within a hair's breadth of tricking her permanently. He'd almost won.

The more fully Kim remembered, the more the blackness that had enveloped her mind lifted, and she was filled with an urgent desire to see Dan again, to touch him, to be with him and with Emily and Betsy.

Pushing back the bedclothes, she reached for the phone. The number was so familiar, it was almost as if it dialed itself. Her heart pounding, Kim listened intently to the ring. John had come so close to making her his prisoner for the rest of her life that she felt a rush of guilt, as though, just by telephoning Dan's home, she was committing a dangerous, daring act. But Kim knew she couldn't think about John now. First she had to find Dan, and then together they would solve all her problems.

The warm, rich voice that she remembered so well broke through her thoughts. Only now it sounded distant, mechanical. "This is

Dr. Dan Stewart. I'm sorry I can't take your call now. If you leave your name and telephone number at the sound of the beep, I will get back to you as soon as I can. If you are a patient, my office will be closed until further notice. I am referring all patients to Dr. Gregory James, telephone number 555-4264."

The receiver fell from Kim's hand. Her worst fears were true. She'd remembered too late. The love that had been buried so deep in her heart poured out in wrenching sobs. Minutes before, she'd been thrilled by the return of her memory. Now those very memories filled her with anguish. Hot tears stung her eyes and poured down her cheeks. Why had Dan given up his practice? What force in his new life could be so powerful that he would turn his back on the very thing that gave it value?

Words he'd once spoken to her came back clearly. "There are three things that give meaning to my life: my children, my practice, and you." Dan had told her that . . . or had he? In her mind Kim could hear him as clearly as if he were speaking now. Yet she was afraid to trust her memory completely. At the same time, she knew she had to. There was nothing else to guide her, no emotional landmarks to show her the way back to her heart. She had to reach him somehow.

"Dan!" Kim murmured his name through

her sobs. Once before he had given up his practice, when Betsy's mother, Liz, had died a week after their wedding. He had loved Liz very deeply. How many times could a man love like that? Kim wasn't sure she wanted to learn the answer. Dan had loved Liz, and he had loved her. Now, could there be a third love in his life? No matter how deep her fears or how hopeless she felt, Kim knew that she had to at least offer Dan her heart again.

It was afternoon when she called again. Gray clouds had covered the sun as she cried her heart out, and the afternoon beyond the shaded windows had become dark and threatening. Somewhere downstairs the woman John had hired to watch over her, more a warden than a nurse, puttered idly, waiting for her to stir. *Any time now she'll be coming to the door to check on me,* Kim thought. Stealthily, she dialed the number she had found etched on her mind. And once again, it was the familiar voice that answered, the voice she yearned to hear, but without the warmth and vibrancy that made her pulse quicken.

This time, she listened intently to every word of the recorded message. When the beep sounded, she was still clutching the receiver, her heart pounding. She knew now what she must do. She'd never be able to escape from her nurse long enough to go to Dan herself. Even if she were free, she wasn't sure she'd have the courage. She would never want to discover firsthand that someone else had taken her place.

At first when she tried to speak, Kim's voice was so hesitant, it was scarcely more than a whisper. Swallowing hard, she forced herself to speak louder. Her voice echoed like a ghost's in the empty, shadowy room. Beginning was the hardest part. She started haltingly, choosing each word as though her life depended on it. Gradually though, her fears and inhibitions receded. Kim told herself that she was talking to Dan, the one man she loved with her whole heart, the husband she had dreamed of, the father whose children she longed to make her own. It was her only chance to speak to him, and within minutes she found herself pouring out her heart as openly and as freely as if he were beside her.

With a wave of her hand and an expansive smile, Susan Stewart dismissed the housekeeper who let her in. "Get on with your packing, Maggie, and don't mind me. I'll entertain myself until Dan and the girls come back."

The housekeeper looked at her watch. "They should be along anytime. Dr. Stewart said no later than two-thirty, and it's way past three already."

"You know how girls are, even at this early age." Susan smiled again, playing the role of indulgent parent, even though she was secretly relieved that Dan was removing Emily from her life again. The child had been a painful intrusion from the day she was born. The only worthwhile thing about Emily in her mother's eyes was the little girl's father. Emily would keep Dan bound to Susan no matter how far afield he wandered. He was the one she'd come to see and to say good-bye to, not the child. "They have to have everything they see or they think they're going to die."

Maggie was shaking her head as she walked away. "I hope they don't come back with another ton of junk. They've already got so much stuff between them, Dr. Stewart will have to charter a plane just to carry it all."

"You should conveniently forget to pack some of it," Susan advised with a knowing, conspiratorial wink. "They'll never miss it, and you'll be doing Dr. Stewart a favor. He'll be indebted to you forever."

"Maybe I will," Maggie agreed sagely. "Those girls will be all the way to Buenos Aires—or wherever it is Dr. Stewart's taking them—before they discover what I left out. And by then, there'll be no way they can blame me."

"That's the spirit, Maggie." Susan laughed and turned away to wait for Dan and Emily to get home.

Being a stranger in her husband's house would never cease feeling odd to her. So many of the things, the furniture and the bric-a-brac, were familiar because they'd been wedding presents or possessions acquired through their married years, she thought as she wandered aimlessly toward the study. In spite of the years they had been divorced, in spite of the fact that Dan had remarried and been widowed since, in spite of the bitterness between them, he would always be her husband, at least in her mind and heart. As far as Susan was concerned, nothing would ever change that.

Now that she was sober again, Susan dared to dream. The one hope that she would never give up was to be Mrs. Dan Stewart again. She knew that Dan admired the way she'd begun to straighten out her life. She would always be an alcoholic, but she would never again allow whiskey to rule her. As long as she kept herself sober, Susan believed that there was still a chance that she and Dan could turn back the clock. She was a part of his life because of Emily, and nothing could ever change that. The bond that united them was unbreakable.

All his deepest ties were right here in Oakdale, she thought complacently. One day Dan would return as surely as he had returned from England. And when he did, who could say what might happen? Although she'd learned how dangerous it was to dream an impossible dream, Susan still cherished a flicker of hope. When that distant time dawned and Dan came home again, she would be a changed woman, sober, together, and very eligible. Without a crystal ball, she could only imagine and dream, but it could come true. One day she might be Mrs. Dan Stewart again—if she made sure that Kim Dixon didn't get in her way. Between them, she and John could use Kim's amnesia to good advantage, Susan thought.

Susan's scheming was cut short by the voice that sounded from the study. "Speak of the devil," she murmured harshly under her breath. She'd recognize Kim Dixon's voice anywhere. But what was she doing here? How could she be talking to Dan?

Tiptoeing closer, Susan listened. She had no compunction about eavesdropping. Yet as she did, an uncomfortable feeling, an odd blend of envy and shame, began creeping over her. Susan had never looked so intimately inside another woman's soul before. It was like hearing someone's confession. Kim was pouring out her deepest, most private emotions—not to Dan, Susan realized, but to his telephone answering machine. A malicious smile turned the corners of Susan's lips. If Kim knew she had an audience, she'd die of embarrassment.

". . . I am beginning to feel again, Dan, and to remember. Through the night and morning, my amnesia has been lifting gradually. I feel like an archaeologist excavating the lost civilization of my mind, carefully, cautiously peeling back layer after layer of personal history, and coming always to the same face, the same feeling, the same man, coming to you and to Emily and Betsy. Kiss them for me, and hold them close.

"When you visited me in the hospital, I felt drawn to you. I didn't understand how or why then. But now I do, and I remember the letter I wrote to you the night before the tornado, explaining everything that was in my heart. I never thought that it and my memory would be lost long before the Valentine's Day that was going to be so specially ours.

"Dan, you know all that was and still is in my heart. There's so much to remember, so much lost time to make up if it's not too late for you, for us. . . ."

Susan had no time to hesitate, no time to weigh the consequences of her actions. Dan and the girls would be walking in at any second. Then her golden opportunity would be lost and Dan with it. Without a second thought, she went into the study, closed the door behind her, and moved swiftly across the room to the desk. Looking at the buttons on the answering machine, she was glad that she was cold sober. For once the small printed letters identifying each function didn't dissolve into an unintelligible blur when she tried to read them. One flick of the reverse/

erase button was all it took. The machine began to whir softly, severing the last possible link between Dan and Kim. Susan watched, a smile of supreme self-satisfaction curling her lips as the words proclaiming Kim's love were erased, wiped out, eradicated forever.

Chapter Eight
A Doctor's Confidence

John Dixon looked out into his waiting room to find it deserted except for a single woman. Good, he thought. There was only one more patient to see before he could go home to Kim. Just knowing his wife was there waiting for him was satisfaction enough. John had no regrets. He'd do it all over again to hold on to Kim.

Picking up the chart from his nurse's desk, he scanned it: Tina Richards, a new patient, age twenty-seven. He glanced up at her again, a skeptical glint in his eye. She looked more like thirty-seven but he'd let the deceit stand until his examination was complete. Under occupation, the woman had written, "Partner, Norman Garrison Enterprises."

When he read that, John's eyebrows lifted

in disbelief. Could there be two Norman Garrisons or was Tina Richards associated with the cardiac patient who had died? Stranger coincidences had occurred. Yet Dixon was too cynical to believe that this woman's visit could be pure happenstance.

Appraising her more carefully, he could see Tina Richards was no angel. She was of medium height with bleached platinum hair down to her shoulders. Her coarse, thick features were coarsened even more by heavy makeup, and she was endowed with the kind of lush figure that made construction workers take off their hardhats and whistle appreciatively.

John Dixon turned back to his office, signaling his nurse with a slight nod.

"Miss Richards," the nurse said crisply, getting up from her desk. "The doctor will see you now. Just walk down to the examining room. It's the first door on your left. Strip completely please and put on a gown, ties in front."

"Hold on there just a minute, miss." Tina had gotten up and slung an oversized tangerine-colored leather pocketbook over her shoulder. "I want to talk to the doc first. That's what I've been sitting here all afternoon for."

"Dr. Dixon likes to have a consultation after the examination," the nurse explained patiently.

"Well, I don't strip just cause a guy snaps

his fingers," she said sharply, "doctor or not. They're all the same, men are. And I've seen enough of them to know." Tina's voice had risen shrilly, and she glanced nervously around the waiting room as though she expected other leering men to spring up from behind the empty chairs and tables at any moment.

"Okay, okay, Miss Richards," the nurse coaxed. "I'm sure Dr. Dixon will be more than happy to talk with you first, if that's what you want." Sitting on the leather couch flipping through the pages of a magazine, Tina Richards had looked like any other patient who was nervous at the prospect of a physical. But once she began to speak, the nurse realized that she was in a state of such high anxiety that the slightest upset could snap her fragile control.

Without any more argument the nurse led the way to Dixon's private office and knocked discreetly. Unless he was conferring with a patient, she usually just rapped once and opened the door. Now though, she waited for him to call, "Come in."

That was signal enough to alert him that something out of the ordinary was up. If any doubt remained in his mind, his nurse's arched brows and wary expression warned him that Tina Richards was not just another patient.

"Miss Richards is very anxious to talk with you before her examination," the nurse said more loudly than she had to. "I assured her that would be agreeable with you, doctor."

"Of course." Dixon nodded readily, but he didn't smile. He was not a man who smiled easily, and now he sensed that he was about to dip into perilous waters.

Once they were alone, Dixon waited for his new patient to sit down and compose herself. Although he knew the odds were against it, he'd been hoping that she'd come for medical reasons only. His nurse's warning expression, though, had told him how foolish he'd been to hope that even momentarily.

Outside, the faltering light of dusk was just beginning to cast the streets in shadows. Kim was probably in the kitchen, he thought, starting their dinner. He'd call her before he left the office, just to check. But first there was Tina Richards to contend with. Wary of what had brought her to his office, he eyed her cautiously.

"You don't know me, doctor, but I know you," she began as she settled herself precariously on the extreme edge of the chair in front of his desk. "At least I know *about* you . . . from being at Oakdale Memorial, I mean."

Leaning back in his swivel chair, Dixon brought his fingertips together and rested his chin on them. "There are many doctors at Oakdale Memorial, Miss Richards," he began smoothly.

"But not many of them have anything to

do with Norman Garrison's case," she interrupted. "Right?"

"I believe Mr. Garrison was a patient of Dr. Hughes," Dixon said, hoping to warn her off. But there was no stopping Tina Richards once she began to unburden herself. In her mind, a doctor was like a priest, and she had come prepared to confess everything, sure that Dr. Dixon would be able to help her.

"Poor Dr. Hughes! That's what I have to tell somebody about, and I know you're in on the case," she insisted.

"I do have a certain interest in it," Dixon conceded. His cool, controlled manner was a sharp contrast to her tense state. Her too bright eyes, her hands that refused to stay still, her high, hysterical tone indicated how very distraught she was.

"That's why I came to you," she rushed on. "Oh, Dr. Dixon, I need your help. I've got to talk to somebody. I don't know what to do. It's such an awful mess. Norman's dead, and it's all my fault. I did it, I know I did. He got so angry I thought he was going to hit me, then all of a sudden, he grabbed at his chest and fell back in the bed, and his eyes. . . . I'll never forget those eyes, rolling up in the back of his head so nothing showed except the whites. I should have kept my big fat trap shut for once, just until he got better. But no." Her voice caught in her throat. "I couldn't wait, and now look at what I've done."

"Miss Richards, please." Dixon had gotten

up from his desk as she spoke and closed the door firmly. "Try to get a grip on yourself. I have no idea what you're talking about or even who you are, let alone why you've come to me. But since you're here, I'm going to listen to what you have to say. Of course I will try to help you if I can."

"I didn't know who else to come to —where to go," she blurted. "Norm made all the decisions, and now . . ."

"Okay, Tina." Dixon sat down in the chair beside her. A premonition grew within him that luck had brought her into his office, and he had no intention of letting her leave until he knew everything that she had to tell. The hospital hearing on the Garrison case was coming up, and he didn't want any embarrassing surprises. "Why don't you begin at the beginning? Who are you, and what exactly was your relationship to Norman Garrison?"

"I'm a businesswoman," she said with definite pride. "Norm and I were partners." Tina hesitated and shot an uncertain look at Dixon, as though she fully expected him to challenge her assertion.

"Partners in what sense?" he asked.

"Oh, I know what you're thinking, doc, and maybe it's true we were that, too. But we were business partners first. On the company books it says I was Norm's private secretary, cause that's how I started. But I was a lot more to him than that. Not that his wife will ever admit it. Norm never made a decision without asking my advice first, and that's the honest truth."

A thin, ironic smile played at the corners of Dixon's lips. "Did he consult you about having a myocardial infarction?"

"Like I said, there wasn't a thing big or small—" Tina began to answer defensively. Then she caught herself. "I get it, doc, you're pulling my leg aren't you?"

Dixon smiled condescendingly. "I'd like very much to hear your story, Tina, but I haven't got all night."

"I know you're very busy," she said apologetically. "I've never met an M.D. yet who wasn't a busy man. So, like I was saying, Norm and I were partners in the business. I guess it kind of spilled over after hours if you know what I mean."

"Garrison was a married man," Dixon reminded her.

"Norm and his wife were on the outs. At least that's what he told me. They were splitting for keeps. Norm wanted to get divorced so he could marry me. That's what he kept saying until he got into the hospital. I don't know what happened to him there." She looked at Dixon questioningly, as if, being a physician, he could explain the inexplicable. When he just sat silently waiting for her to get on with her story, she shrugged in helpless puzzlement. "Norm changed, that's for sure. Beats me how it happened. The guy gets sick, and all of a sudden he doesn't want anything to do with me. Doesn't even want me to go visit him. It was like he was embarrassed or something. I had to sneak in late at night after visiting hours so nobody would see me. How do you think that made me feel after all I'd done for Norm?"

Dixon looked curiously at the distraught woman beside him. Clearly Tina Richards thought she had had Norman Garrison wrapped up in a neat little package. But Garrison hadn't been quite the chump he'd pretended to be. "Did you tell Garrison how you felt?" he questioned, sensing that they were getting close to the heart of the matter that had brought the woman to his office.

"Of course I did. I was madder than I've ever been in my life."

"Mad enough to kill?" Dixon's damning question was posed in a soft, quiet voice, and for an instant it seemed as if Tina hadn't understood it. Then suddenly she stared at him with wild, frightened eyes.

"I didn't kill him. I swear on my mother's grave, I didn't. I felt like I could, but I didn't touch him—and that's the honest truth. He just sat up and—" Tina's voice broke, and she buried her face in her hands, too frightened even to cry. "You've got to believe me, doc," she pleaded. "I loved the guy. I really loved the guy."

"I believe you, Tina," Dixon replied with convincing sincerity in his tone. "And I want to help you every way I can. But you've got to get a hold on yourself and tell me exactly what happened. You went to visit Norman at the hospital late one night after visiting hours. Is that right?"

She nodded mutely without lifting her head and he went on. "The night Norman Garrison died. But Dr. Hughes was in the room with him so you didn't go in."

"No! No it wasn't like that." Tina stared up at him, too upset to realize that Dixon was trying to give her an airtight alibi and make her a witness against Bob. "There was nobody in Norm's room. He was lying in the bed alone. At first I thought he was asleep, but when I tiptoed in, he opened his eyes and said, 'What are *you* doing here?' Just like that, as if I was nobody."

"Are you sure—" Dixon tried to interrupt, but once Tina had begun to unburden herself she couldn't stop. The story poured out like a flood.

"'I came to see you, Norm. I've been so worried about you.' That's what I said. He looked at me as if I was dirt, some tart he'd picked up for the night. 'You've got no business coming around here. What if somebody sees you?' he said. I couldn't believe my own ears. 'It's me, Tina. Remember, honey? I love you, Norm. We're getting married just as soon as you get out of here,' I said. And you know what he did, doc? He looked at me—me all dolled up in a new outfit, my hair just permed—he looked at me and he laughed. 'Wake up, Tina,' he said. 'Just cause I'm in the hospital, it doesn't mean I'm sick in the head. I'm married already, remember?'

"That's when I got mad, doc, so mad that I wanted to kill him. He never loved me, not for a minute. He was just like all the others but he had me fooled, fooled real good." A long, angry shudder flowed through her. "I guess I lost my head. I can't remember word for word what I said, but I called him every name in the book. He kept telling me to shut up. He didn't even care what I was saying. He was just afraid somebody would hear us. But I wouldn't stop. I couldn't. I wanted everyone to hear what kind of a bastard Norman Garrison was, the nurses and the doctors and his wife, all of them. I swore I was going to tell them all, to keep on screaming until they all heard.

"That's when Norm sat up in bed with this awful expression on his face as if he was really going to get out of bed and kill me with his bare hands. 'I'm going to make you shut up,' he yelled and he tried to grab for me, but I ducked away. That's when he grabbed at his chest and fell back on the bed. I got scared. 'Norm,' I cried, 'Norm.' But his eyes rolled up in the back of his head and his mouth fell open. I got so scared, doc, I ran out of there as fast as I could. I remember brushing by somebody in the hall, but I was too upset to see who it was."

Tina paused, trying to regain control of herself. Just telling the story was almost like living through it again. Still it felt better to finally get it off her chest. And John Dixon was a doctor. He'd be able to tell her the right thing to do.

Dixon was looking at her critically, trying to gauge the best way to control Tina Richards. He had to convince her to keep silent. If her testimony ever came out before Bob Hughes's hearing, it would be disastrous. Dixon desperately wanted Bob to be convicted. He had hated him for years and had never forgiven him for his affair with Kim. Now, at last, John would have the revenge he craved. All he had to do was keep Tina Richards from talking.

"Why didn't you go to the police when you heard that Garrison was dead?" Dixon demanded.

"The police!" Tina gasped with renewed fear. "But I didn't kill Norm. I never touched him. I loved him," she blurted, becoming hysterical again.

"Then why did you come here? Why are you telling me all this?"

Tina stared up at him, her eyes deep wells of fear. "It's just that I saw in the paper about Dr. Hughes and the hearing at the hospital. He shouldn't have to take the rap for me."

"Then you have no choice but to go to the police and confess that you caused Norman Garrison to have a lethal heart attack," Dixon stated grimly. "Is that what you want?"

Tina was shaking her head fiercely. "I can't

do that. I can't go to the cops. What if they throw the book at me?"

"I have no doubt they would," Dixon answered dryly, "and I don't know how becoming a striped suit would be on you." He paused thoughtfully, as if considering the issue seriously. "No, Tina, you wouldn't have much sympathy on your side. A married man and a very sick one at that being harassed by a grasping, ambitious secretary. It doesn't look good, no matter what the truth really is. You know how the papers and the TV can twist a story like yours."

Tina's face had gone deathly pale as Dixon talked, and all she could do was repeat, "No! No!" in a terrified whisper.

Leaning over, he patted her arm reassuringly. "Under the circumstances, Tina, my best advice is to keep your nose out of it. Don't get involved or you may be facing a murder rap yourself."

"But Dr. Hughes . . ." Tina began to protest.

"Bob Hughes is only facing a hospital hearing, not a legal murder charge. And what's more, he's very capable of defending himself," Dixon said easily. "So there's nothing at all for you to worry or feel guilty about. If you know what's good for you, you won't breathe a word to anyone about your visit with Garrison or this conversation. And I'll do my best to forget that I ever saw you today. Trust me, Tina," he said, squeezing her arm again and speaking in his best professional manner. "I'd hate to see a good woman like yourself paying with the best years of her life for a crime that never even happened. Remember, you have nothing to feel guilty about. Just leave it to me. All you have to do is try to forget Norman Garrison."

Tina nodded as trustingly as a child. Doctors always knew best. At least that's what she'd been brought up to believe.

John Dixon was smiling to himself as he escorted Tina to the door. Until her confession there had always been a worry in the back of his mind that someone might come forward to get Bob Hughes off the hook, but now that wouldn't happen. At least he was going to nail Hughes's hide to the hospital wall and make him pay for being the first man to claim Kim. Dixon had waited a long time for his revenge, and now that it was at hand, he wanted to see Bob Hughes suffer.

Chapter Nine
Call to Judgment

Draping an arm casually across the back of his chair, John Dixon looked around the hospital conference room and crossed his legs, making sure not to wrinkle his iron-gray gabardine slacks. Although it was supposed to be an informal hearing, the room was arranged very much like a courtroom. The four men serving as judges—Dixon, the hospital administrator and two members of the board—were seated at a long table which was empty except for a tray with a water pitcher and four glasses, as well as a yellow legal pad and freshly-sharpened pencils at each place.

At a much smaller table facing them sat Bob Hughes, flanked on his right by an empty chair. Behind him in a row of straight chairs were the nurse and resident who'd been on duty the night of Norman Garrison's fatal heart attack, and his widow, Sandy, dressed in a straight black dress with white collar and cuffs.

The administrator who was chairing the hearing coughed self-consciously. "Dr. Hughes, if you're ready," he began in a suitably grave voice, "I'd like to start this hearing by reviewing the events of the evening in question."

Bob Hughes, his face gray from the grueling ordeal he was being subjected to so soon after his wife's tragic death, nodded despondently. He'd hoped that his son Tom would be at his side to give him moral support as well as legal expertise, but Tom and his new wife Natalie had been away on a cruise when Norman Garrison had died. In fact they'd just gotten back the night before and a heavy caseload had built up in their absence. With a deep sigh of regret, Bob tried to concentrate on the administrator's words.

"If you have no objections, Dr. Hughes," he said, "I'd like to begin by asking you to describe for us the condition of the patient, Norman Garrison, when you admitted him to Oakdale Memorial."

"Norman Garrison had never been a patient of mine. In fact I'd never met the man before he came to the hospital," Bob began candidly.

"Very unusual, wouldn't you say, doctor?" John Dixon interrupted sharply. "In view of the circumstances, I think we'd all like to know how you came to admit a total stranger and accept him as a private patient."

Bob grimaced. He should have expected as much from Dixon, but he was still caught unprepared. Looking from one of his judges to the other, he spoke haltingly. "As Dr. Dixon very well knows, Mrs. Garrison and I were married once many years ago. When her husband was stricken suddenly with a myocardial infarction, she quite naturally turned to the only doctor she knew, and that happened to be me."

While Bob was speaking, Tom Hughes slipped into the hearing room and took the chair beside his father. He'd had no time to study the details of the case let alone work out a line of defense, still he wanted to be with his father at the inquiry. For Tom's entire life, his father had been beside him when he needed him most. Now it was time for him to show his appreciation. Seeing Tom, Bob smiled proudly and shook his son's hand.

"Sorry I'm late, Dad," Tom whispered. But Bob was already listening to the next speaker. The administrator was calling on the resident to give his account of the evening of Garrison's death. As Bob had expected, the testimony was damning, and when Claire Browning was called on to corroborate it, the case appeared to be all sewn up. There wasn't very much Bob could say to defend himself. It was their word against his, and they had no reason to be prejudiced against him. Bob's head slumped against his chest in despair. Norman Garrison was dead, and he was being held responsible.

But Sandy Garrison couldn't sit by silently and watch Bob's career being destroyed because of Norman and her.

"Excuse me!" She found herself on her feet, demanding to be heard.

"Mrs. Garrison." The administrator was clearly taken aback by her unexpected interruption. "Is there something you have to add to these proceedings?"

"Yes . . . yes, there is." She faltered. Now that she had actually gained their attention, she wasn't even sure what she was going to say. All she knew with certainty was that she had to protect Bob. "I realize now," she began haltingly, "that I should have come forward right away—as soon as my husband was pronounced dead—and explained everything. But all I can say is that in the shock of his passing, I didn't want to remember anything but the happy parts of my marriage."

The administrator leaned across the table, a puzzled, disturbed expression on his face. "I'm not sure my colleagues or I understand what you're trying to tell us."

Swallowing hard, Sandy looked him squarely in the face. "The person this doctor and nurse heard arguing with my husband was not Dr. Hughes. I was with Norman that night—alone with him—and we . . . we got into an argument. I don't remember how it started, probably over something trivial, the way it usually does with a husband and wife, but—"

"No, Sandy!" Bob Hughes had swiveled around and now was pleading with her to stop. "I won't let you perjure yourself for my sake."

"Dad!" Tom tried to interrupt, but his father ignored him.

"I'm very grateful to Mrs. Garrison for trying to spare me," he said turning back to face his judges, "but I can't allow her to lie for me. Please strike from the record of this hearing everything she has just told you. It was all a fabrication, invented to save my name and my reputation."

"I'm sorry, Bob." Sandy sank back into her chair weeping. "So sorry for everything."

"A touching scene, and a very enlightening one," John Dixon said mockingly. "And in view of it, I'd like to ask Mrs. Garrison a question. Isn't it true, Mrs. Garrison, that your husband believed you and Dr. Hughes were considerably more than ex-husband and wife?"

"I'm not sure I understand," Sandy began uncertainly.

"Let me make it clearer then," Dixon said. "Norman Garrison believed that you and Dr. Hughes were having an affair, even while he lay incapacitated in his hospital bed. Judging from the touching little scene we have all witnessed, it seems obvious that Garrison's suspicions were more than justified. Clearly Mrs. Garrison's behavior this morning is that of a woman who feels something considerably more than innocent friendship for Dr. Hughes." Dixon finished speaking and settled back smugly, confident that he had accomplished his every aim. In trying to spare each other, Sandy and Bob had played directly into his vengeful hands.

Although Tom Hughes jumped up, shouting objections to Dixon's innuendoes, the administrator ignored his outbreak. Satisfied that all the parties had been allowed ample opportunity to speak, the four judges went into conference.

While they waited for the verdict, Tom and Sandy tried to make small talk to distract Bob, but their efforts were futile. The hearing hadn't gone well, and he knew it. His career, his profession, all he had left in life besides his little daughter, hung in the balance. The minutes dragged like hours.

"At least they're talking. It's not cut and dry," Sandy kept repeating hopefully. "Don't you think that's a good sign, Tom? The longer they take . . ."

Tom shrugged, dampening her optimism. He'd sat in too many courtrooms to try to guess what was going on behind the closed doors, and he didn't want to give his father false hope.

Behind them the resident and nurse murmured in low tones, like mourners at a wake. But Bob didn't seem to notice. He appeared locked in his own thoughts. Sitting as motionless as a statue, he let the desultory conversation drift around him like a cloud.

Finally the judges returned, grim-faced, and took their places again.

"Dr. Hughes." The administrator picked up a sheaf of papers then put them down again and looked over the table at Bob. "We have all given this case our most careful consideration. I would be less than forthright if I did not say that Mr. Garrison's death has caused this hospital grave concern. Throughout its long and estimable history, Memorial Hospital has prided itself on employing a staff of physicians who always put the well-being of their patients above personal considerations.

"In this case we feel you exhibited a certain, most unfortunate, lapse of self-control. It is not our position or intention to cast censure on your personal relationship with the patient or his wife. We are not moral watchdogs. However, Dr. Hughes, when, through his personal feelings, a doctor jeopardizes the life or the health of a patient in this hospital, then we cannot simply close our eyes. Here at Memorial Hospital our first obligation is to the patient. Therefore, it is the decision of this board that you failed to serve Norman Garrison with the impartial care and dedication we expect from our medical staff. It is not for us to say whether, under another doctor's auspices, Mr. Garrison might still be alive today. But neither can we condone your behavior. In the opinion of this board you allowed personal feelings to get out of control, with the most unfortunate results.

"Thanks to Mrs. Garrison's understanding this hospital will not be sued for malpractice. But that does not exonerate your behavior. In view of the long and excellent service you have provided Memorial Hospital in the past, we will not suspend you from the staff, Dr. Hughes. However, we trust that you will take this decision as a most severe reprimand for your handling of the Norman Garrison case. You failed your patient and your hospital. A second incident like this cannot and will not be forgiven."

The tension in the conference room was almost palpable when he finished. The two other board members looked soberly at some vacant spot above the heads of their audience; a certain smugness showed in their expressions as if they were satisfied with the outcome of the hearing. By contrast, John Dixon appeared irritated and impatient with the administrator's long-winded speech. It was a partial victory, but Dixon had wanted much more. He'd wanted to watch Bob Hughes hang. Instead Bob was walking away with little more than a slap on the wrist.

If Dixon thought the verdict was too mild, Bob Hughes heard it very differently. His face, which had been white and expressionless throughout the hearing, turned a deep, angry red as the administrator spoke. He'd given the best years of his life to Oakdale Memorial Hospital. He'd always put his patients first, even before his family. He was absolutely blameless, and this was the thanks he got. How much worse could it be to be thrown off the staff?

Bob had no intention of hanging around, waiting to find out. Blind with fury, he pushed back his chair and stood up. "Come on, son," he muttered through clenched teeth. "I want to get out of here. And I never want to set foot inside this place again for the rest of my life."

Holding back his own anger and the pain he felt for his father, Tom stood up, prouder and straighter than he ever had before. "Don't worry, Dad," he swore quietly. "We haven't even begun to fight yet."

But Bob wasn't listening. He'd already made up his mind what he was going to do.

Chapter Ten
Paradise Lost

The days and weeks turned into a silent, seamless nightmare, and still Kim waited. Mornings and nights merged. There was no brightness in her life, no light of hope, only the darkness of despair, the black void of an empty heart.

Dan was gone and she was free. Once he was safely out of Oakdale, John had let up his guard. He had no fear of losing Kim anymore, but she still lived as if she were his prisoner. Her freedom had come too late. Just as her memory had. If Dan still loved her, he would have stayed in Oakdale, answered the cry of her heart, rushed to her. Instead there had been an unbearable abyss of silence. Her message of love had fallen on deaf ears, or so she believed.

Kim prayed for a second tornado to strike

her. She had no reason left to live and no desire to remember. Looking back, she wished her amnesia had never lifted. Without memories, there had been no pain, no heartbreak. But now it was impossible to forget and a torment to remember. Her heart wept for Dan and the girls and for the life they'd never share now. How cruel fate had been to make her remember what was better forgotten. Old friends, like Bob Hughes, scarcely recognized the depressed, withdrawn woman Kim had become. Even in the worst of times she had always been energetic, vivacious, outgoing, full of life and fun. The change was startling. But Bob was too mired in his own problems to offer much help to his sister-in-law. And of course, there was John to contend with.

In contrast to his wife, John had never been happier. He had what he wanted. Kim belonged to him again. He showered her with presents, a new car, a full-length mink coat, expensive jewelry. Although she accepted the gifts graciously, they meant nothing to her because they had been given by the wrong man. She knew she should talk to John and explain how she felt. Instead she kept postponing the confrontation. It seemed pointless now and frightening. She knew she should leave John, but without Dan where would she go? What would she do? Disappointment and fear held her hostage, making it impossible to take any action big or small. She couldn't even find a way to refuse John when he turned to her in bed. No matter how many late, late movies she watched on TV, no matter how much she stalled before finally giving into her body's demand for sleep, he was always awake, and usually waiting for her. The moment she lay down, his hands began fumbling with her nightgown.

"Please, John," she'd murmur, hoping to dissuade him yet knowing that nothing would. Inevitably, he'd become even more demanding. In the early years of their marriage, when Kim had begged him for children, he'd refused even to consider the idea. A baby would demand her attention and steal her love. John was too jealous, too possessive to share her with anyone. A long time ago Kim had accepted the fact that the only children she was ever going to have were Emily and Betsy. Now even they had been swept out of her life.

I feel so terribly alone and desperate, Kim thought one bleak afternoon as she sat in her doctor's waiting room, flipping through a six-month-old issue of *Time* magazine and looking surreptitiously at the other women, most of them in various stages of pregnancy, who were also waiting to be examined. It wasn't that she was envious of them. A baby now was the last thing she wanted to bring to a marriage that had been a mistake from the beginning. Still, she couldn't deny the sense of loss she felt as she looked at them. Having a baby is such a natural part of being a woman that everyone assumes she can and will be a mother one day.

"Mrs. Dixon?" The nurse's call interrupted her thoughts. Getting up quickly, she followed the white-uniformed figure through the narrow corridor to an examining room. Kim felt more like a hypochondriac with every step. There was probably nothing at all wrong with her, except depression; and there was only one doctor in the world who could cure that. But she was due for an annual checkup anyway. She'd missed a couple of periods, and she always felt tired. Some days she didn't want to get up at all.

Taking off her street clothes and putting on an examining gown, she lay down on the table and steeled herself for the internal examination. If the gynecologist weren't a friend of John's, it wouldn't be so embarrassing, she thought as Dr. George Kurias came in, a smile on his ruddy face.

"Well, Kim, anything special the matter or are you just in for a routine checkup?" he asked as he washed his hands.

"Just routine," she lied. "Nothing's the matter, but I'm overdue for a checkup."

"Glad to hear it. And how's John? We haven't bumped into each other lately. Funny how things go. Sometimes we see each other in the hospital a couple of times a day. Other times we don't lay eyes on each other for a week or more."

Brusque and cheerful, Dr. Kurias carried on an easy line of small talk as he examined Kim.

"We should get together some evening now that you're feeling better," he said amiably. "You and John and my wife and I could go out to dinner and—" He broke off in mid-sentence, pressing more firmly on her abdomen. "Are you sure you only came in for a routine examination?" he asked guardedly.

Kim nodded, although she couldn't help noticing the sudden change in the doctor's tone. A serious frown had replaced his pleasant smile, and his manner became grave.

"I don't want to say anything definitely until we do some tests," he said in his best professional voice, "but it looks to me as though you're going to have quite a bit to talk to your husband about tonight."

By the time John got home from the hospital, Kim was numb with shock. Just minutes before he walked through the door, the doctor's office called with the test results, leaving her white and shaken.

"Hi, darling. I hope you haven't slaved over dinner because I thought—" John started cheerfully as he came in. But one look at Kim's ashen face and he stopped short. "What's the matter? Do you feel sick? You're as pale as a ghost," he said. Rushing over to the wing chair where she sat as motionless as a statue, he took her wrist and checked her pulse, concern etched deeply in his sharp, narrow face.

"I'm fine, John," she murmured. "I mean, I'm not sick the way you think." She faltered, unable or unwilling to meet his anxious gaze. "I went to the doctor today, George Kurias."

"Is anything the matter?" he asked. "You didn't tell me you had an appointment."

"I didn't want to worry you." She stopped and inhaled deeply, trying desperately to gain control of her confused, conflicting emotions. "I just haven't been feeling like myself lately, and I was overdue for a checkup."

"Well I trust George gave you a clean bill of health. If there was anything radically wrong he would have called me himself," John answered confidently.

Clasping her hands to steady herself, Kim took a deep breath and swallowed hard. "I guess he thought I should tell you this myself," she murmured uncertainly. "His office just called with the results of the tests he did. I don't know how to tell you this, John," she admitted, shrinking back into the chair. Her mouth felt as dry as if she were lost in a desert, and a fine line of sweat formed over her lip. "It's not happy news . . . at least not for us," she stammered.

"What is it, darling?" John coaxed. "You said you're not sick."

"Not sick," Kim repeated blankly. "I'm not sick. I'm . . . I don't know how to tell you, John. I can't believe it myself after all these years."

John grinned triumphantly. "You're pregnant, Kim! That's it, isn't it? I should have guessed right away. We'll open a bottle of champagne."

Kim stared at him as if she were seeing a total stranger. "You mean you don't mind, John? You want this baby?"

"Want our baby?" he laughed sharply. "Of course I do. It's perfect. Just what we need."

"But all these years," Kim began, unable to disguise her disbelief, "you've refused to even consider having children."

"I used to feel that way," John conceded readily. "But a man can change, can't he? We're both older now, more mature, more responsible."

"You're serious, aren't you?" she broke in incredulously. "You really do want this baby?"

Kneeling down beside her, John took both her hands and held them in his. "I want it for you, darling," he murmured slyly. "I think it's exactly what our marriage needs." And for once he spoke the truth. It wasn't an accident that Kim had gotten pregnant. It was exactly what he had planned. It was the final, irreversible step in his scheme to complete his control over her. It was true. For years the very idea of a child coming into their life had filled him with jealousy. But now he realized that a baby was the one thing that would tie Kim to him forever. How could she even think about leaving him now that she was carrying his child?

John laughed out loud, pleased with his own cleverness. "Don't move, darling," he ordered, giving her hands a final squeeze. "I'm going to open that champagne. This is the happiest day of our new life together."

Watching him walk toward the kitchen, Kim felt anything but happy. She wanted a baby, but she wanted one conceived in love. She wanted Dan's baby. Instead it was John's. The new life that was just beginning to form was like the final toll of fate, locking her permanently into a loveless marriage. Even as the child took shape within her, the last flicker of hope was snuffed out. Now Kim was sure she'd never escape from John Dixon.

Chapter Eleven

Guilty Until Proven Innocent

"You did what, Dad?" Tom Hughes couldn't believe his ears. His father was sitting opposite him at the best steakhouse in town, calmly slicing into a prime porterhouse steak.

Bob took a bite of the very rare beef and chewed it slowly and thoroughly before answering. "I resigned from the hospital. I sent a letter to the board of directors this morning telling them of my decision."

"But you can't do that, Dad," Tom insisted, pushing his plate away before he'd even taken a bite.

"I can't do anything else—after that hearing," he corrected sharply. "How could I ever walk down the hall of Oakdale Memorial Hospital again?"

"I never thought my father was a quitter," Tom snapped back, shaking his head in anger and disbelief.

"What else can I do?" Bob asked, forcing himself to go on eating as if the whole miserable business meant little or nothing to him. He didn't want anyone to see how devastated the decision had left him. Nothing, except Jennifer's death, had ever caused him so much anguish.

"You could stand up and fight back like a man," Tom answered more harshly than he'd intended. "You could show John Dixon and his friends that they tried to jerk the wrong man around."

Bob Hughes put down his knife and fork and stared intently at his son. Around them the steakhouse buzzed with the intense, spirited talk of the business-lunch crowd. The Guernsey Steakhouse was a favorite spot in downtown Oakdale. The decor was attractive, with dark red lacquered walls, rough-hewn wooden tables and Tiffany style lamps; and the menu consisted of the best steaks available, perfectly grilled over hickory logs, fresh salads and potatoes. It was a businessman's paradise.

"To tell you the truth, Tom," he said, suddenly feeling older and more tired than he ever had before, "I don't think I have the stomach for a fight. I'm bowing out, and that's all there is to it."

"But I thought you were innocent." Tom persisted. "Garrison was already dead when you walked into his room, wasn't he?"

Bob nodded.

"Well, I've got to tell you, Dad, you're saying one thing, and acting as if you don't believe it yourself. If you resign from the hospital now with this cloud hanging over your head, you might as well take out a full-page ad in the Sunday paper that says Guilty as Charged. Because that's the message you're giving loud and clear to everybody in Oakdale."

Even as Tom argued, his father was shaking his head in defeat. "Don't you see, Tom, it doesn't matter anymore. My name, my reputation, my word have already been destroyed."

"Well, if you don't care for yourself, the least you can do is think of your family," Tom persisted. "How do you think it's going to be for Frannie growing up with that cloud over her? How will she ever be able to hold her head up in this town if you can't?"

Bob's fingers tightened so violently around the knife and fork that his knuckles turned white. Frannie was all he had left in the world, his only reason to get up in the morning. If she couldn't look up to him, if she even came to despise him he didn't know what he'd do. The thought was too agonizing even to hold in his mind for a moment. "You know I want Frannie to have the best of everything," he murmured in a voice thick with emotion.

"Including a father she can look up to and respect?" Tom asked.

Bob nodded grimly.

"Then you've got to fight back, Dad." Tom pressed his advantage. When his father didn't put up an argument, he went ahead, plotting a counterattack. "For starters, you've got to withdraw that rash, impetuous resignation right away. Say you were so upset over the hearing that you lost your head. Say anything, just as long as you get the letter back, okay?"

"I'll do whatever I have to," Bob agreed. But it was clear from his face and his voice that he thought Tom had embarked on a losing battle. He had little faith and less hope that the verdict against him could ever be reversed and his good name restored in the community.

"Good," Tom said crisply, ignoring his father's pessimism. "The next thing we have to do is prove your innocence by reconstructing exactly the night of Garrison's death."

"I told you what happened," Bob said impatiently. "I went to the hospital late—it must have been around ten-thirty—to check on my patients because I couldn't sleep. It was so quiet at home, I had to get away. To avoid waiting interminably for the public elevator, I took the back elevator. When I got to the hall where Garrison's room was, someone was hurrying toward me. The corridor was dim. Just the night lights were on, and I was preoccupied I suppose. Anyway, I didn't even notice if it was a man or woman. All that registered clearly in my mind was a fur coat brushing past me. Then I think I heard the fire-stairs door open as I went into Garrison's room. He was already dead when I arrived. I'd stake my entire career on that. A few seconds after I arrived, the resident and the nurse rushed in."

"You're sure that's exactly how it was, Dad?" Tom had pulled out a leather-bound notebook from his breast pocket while his father was talking and had begun to jot down notes. "There's nothing else you can remember? No detail, even if it seems very insignificant?"

"That's everything I know, Tom." Bob sounded apologetic. If he'd had the foresight to know that the night was going to be such a critical one in his life, he would have paid more attention.

"It's fine, Dad," Tom said encouragingly, "but it's just the beginning, a first step. We've got to get a record of everybody who was working on the floor that night, and we have to interview each one. With luck and enough persistence, maybe we'll find someone who remembers something that didn't come out in the hearing."

"But the resident and nurse who testified

are convinced they heard me arguing with Garrison," Bob reminded him bleakly. "You'll never be able to change their minds."

"Circumstantial evidence," Tom said with more conviction than he felt. "They probably did hear someone arguing and, when they found you in the room, they assumed it was you. It all fit so neatly. Garrison was fighting with his wife's ex-husband who also happened to be his doctor. It was easy to jump to conclusions."

"You know that, and I know that," Bob pointed out, "But the rest of the world doesn't."

"You just get that resignation letter back and leave the rest of the world to me," Tom answered heartily. "But first what do you say to a piece of rhubarb pie for dessert? We're going to need all the strength we can get to win this one."

Tom massaged his temples with his fingers and tried to block out Natalie's litany of complaints. According to her, things had deteriorated drastically since their marriage. Before they were married it seemed as if he had all the time in the world for Natalie. But somehow since the wedding, he'd been tied up night and day in case after case. And now with his father's name to clear as well, he was working eighteen and sometimes twenty-hour days.

Tom sighed guiltily. Natalie had every right

to complain, still it was tough to listen to, especially so early in the morning. Four hours of sleep had not been enough to fortify him for her onslaught. And in any case, he was so preoccupied with trying to prove his father's innocence that he wouldn't have been able to concentrate on what she was saying even if he'd had eight solid hours of sleep and a pot of strong, black coffee.

A week had passed since Bob Hughes had withdrawn his resignation. Still, Tom was no closer to exonerating his father than he'd been the day they had eaten lunch together. Every lead had fizzled. It seemed that no one on duty that night had heard or seen anything that could help Bob. Tom was beginning to think he might be facing a conspiracy of silence. But why? Who would want to ruin his father, except possibly the vindictive John Dixon.

Assuring himself that there was still hope, Tom gulped a second cup of coffee and blew a kiss in Natalie's direction, deaf to the fact that she was still telling him how neglected she felt. A half slice of freshly buttered toast flew after him as he dashed out, but the angry effort was wasted. The moment he'd stood up from the breakfast table, Tom had put his marital troubles behind him and focused all his attention on the nurse he was going to interview.

He glanced at his watch. It was a quarter to eight. In fifteen minutes she'd be coming off her shift. There was just time enough to get to the hospital and intercept her. Hannah Davis was the last person he had to speak to. She'd been on private duty for the past couple of weeks, preventing Tom from talking to her sooner. But if the hospital records were in order, she had been working on the eleventh floor the night that Norman Garrison died.

Stationing himself at the main entrance, he waited for her to come off her shift. In a phone call the day before the nurse had described herself as "a blonde mom, on the slim side, I hope, sort of the June Allison type. At least that's what people always tell me."

When he saw her hesitate at the door and glance around for him, Tom thought how perfectly Hannah Davis had described herself. "Mrs. Davis?" he said, approaching her with his hand extended.

"Hannah," she said, smiling and shaking hands warmly. "You must be Dr. Hughes's son. Your father is a wonderful man."

Tom exhaled a sigh of relief. Clearly Hannah Davis was a friendly witness which made his job much easier. "I think my dad's a pretty wonderful guy," he admitted, returning her smile. "But these days it seems as if we're a minority of two."

"Is it really that bad?" Hannah's bright face clouded. "I've got to confess I've barely glanced at a newspaper or television these past few weeks. I've been so busy trying to juggle four kids and take care of a terminal cancer patient, it hasn't left much time for anything else. And being on private duty, I haven't gotten the usual hospital gossip. This is my first day back on staff. I guess I told you that on the phone."

"Let's grab a cup of coffee, and I'll fill you in on what's been going on between my dad and Oakdale Memorial. It's not a pretty story, but then I guess, I'm not the most objective person in the world."

An hour and several cups of coffee later, Tom and Hannah were still huddled together in a corner booth of a nearby diner. After listening intently to Tom's rundown, Hannah began to reconstruct her own memories aloud.

"I do remember that night," she said, nodding her head for emphasis, "because I was so worried. My husband had to go out of town unexpectedly on business and I didn't have a chance to switch shifts. So I had to leave the kids alone. My oldest is fifteen and very responsible. Still, I don't like to leave them at night. To make matters worse, I had to act as floor nurse because the regular called in sick. She'd gone out to dinner and gotten food poisoning. You've got to be very careful with shellfish, especially out of season.

"Anyway," Hannah went on, apologizing with her eyes for digressing, "that's why I was in charge that night. I remember Mr. Garrison well. You always remember the difficult patients, and he certainly was a demanding one. He made us nurses earn our pay every night. His wife was a different sort. She was very polite and considerate, but he was too much for her to handle if you ask me."

"Tell me exactly what you remember about the night Garrison died," Tom coached, trying to focus her attention. "Did you check on him yourself at any point?"

"Sure I did." Hannah nodded vigorously. "I checked his vital signs just before I went on my break around ten o'clock. And I didn't see Dr. Hughes. He certainly wasn't in Mr. Garrison's room when I checked him. Come to think of it, I didn't see Dr. Hughes at all until I got back. He was on the phone then, at the nurses' station, and he seemed very upset."

"We'll come back to my father," Tom promised. "But first tell me, how was Garrison the last time you saw him?"

"Resting comfortably," Hannah answered confidently. "At least as comfortably as a man like that can. He wasn't used to sitting still, let alone being confined to a hospital bed, and it was hard for him. I didn't much like the man to tell the truth," she admitted, the hint of a flush coloring her cheeks. "But I did feel kind of sorry for him. It was tough not to. He was like a big bear in a cage."

"Then when you left him around ten o'clock," Tom said, reconstructing the facts carefully, "Norman Garrison gave no indication that he was a man only minutes away from death?"

"None whatsoever," Hannah agreed promptly. She would, Tom noted, make a very convincing witness.

"And he was alone in his hospital room, resting but not asleep?" Tom continued.

Hannah cocked a knowing eyebrow at him. "Well, that's right, I guess, at least as far as it goes."

"What do you mean?" he inquired, feeling his pulse quicken suddenly. There *was* something else, something that no one had revealed yet. He was sure of it, but he didn't want to put words into Hannah's mouth.

She shrugged indifferently. "I don't imagine it's even worth mentioning, but you know Mr. Garrison was always having visitors after hours. It didn't matter a bit to him what the hospital rules were. 'Rules are made to be broken.' That's what he'd always say when I warned him. Never paid the slightest attention. You'd think it was his personal hotel, he acted so high and mighty."

Tom was so tense with apprehension he could barely force the words out of his mouth. "On the night he died, did Garrison have any after-hour visitors?"

"Just the usual." Hannah shot Tom a knowing glance. "It was always the same every night I was on duty."

"A woman?" Tom asked unnecessarily. "Can you describe her?"

Hannah shook her head. "That kind all looks the same to me, if you know what I'm saying. But her coat—that I won't forget. Sable or something, and full-length. A real knockout. It must have set Garrison back a pretty penny."

"Do you think you'd recognize her if you saw her again?" Tom asked hopefully.

"The woman?" Hannah frowned. "I'm not sure I'd recognize her. But I'd certainly recognize the coat. It had this enormous collar that she used to wear up around her neck, with her hair tucked inside it. The collar alone would have cost me a year's salary."

Moments after leaving Hannah Davis in the diner parking lot, Tom was seated in Sandy Garrison's living room, asking if her husband had ever given her a fur coat.

"That's an unusual question to spring on a widow first thing in the morning." Sandy smiled and curled up in one corner of the sofa. On the end table beside her was a large, full-color photograph of her late husband matted and framed in sterling silver. "Can I get you a cup of coffee?" she offered graciously.

"If I even look at another cup of coffee today, I'll start floating away," Tom assured her.

"Can I interest you in anything except a fur coat?" she teased gently.

"I know it must sound like a bizarre question," Tom said apologetically. "But please trust me. Believe me, I wouldn't be bothering you if it weren't very, very important."

"I do trust you." Sandy smiled again. "You're Bob Hughes's son, and that's reason enough for me. But to answer your question, Norman gave me several fur coats through the years. He was generous that way. He loved giving presents to everyone. Norman was the kind of guy who thought a gift could make up for the way he treated you, which was usually pretty lousy. Nothing I ever said convinced him that life just doesn't work that way."

Although he didn't want to cut her off, Tom was anxious to identify Norman Garrison's night caller. "Do you mind describing the coats to me? Or better yet, could I take a look at them?"

Sandy gave him a questioning look, but she complied readily enough. If it helped Bob to show his son her fur coats, then she'd do it, unusual though the request was. Leading the way into the bedroom she'd once shared with her husband, Sandy slid open mirrored doors to reveal an enormous walk-in closet. Tom stifled the urge to whistle in astonishment. He'd never seen so many clothes except in a store. Sandy hadn't been joking when she said her husband had been generous. There were row upon row of dresses suitable for every season and occasion. On one rack, which stretched from wall to wall, there were a dozen furs of various colors and styles.

To Sandy's surprise Tom flicked through

them with lightning speed, then turned back to her, disappointment clear in his eyes. "Is this all?" he asked.

"Don't you think it's enough?" she answered dryly. "I am only one woman after all."

Tom stared blankly at the line of furs. The longest one was a three-quarter length beige mink. "I was hoping you had a full-length fur," he admitted, "with an enormous collar to bundle up in. Something very exotic, a real eye-catcher."

Sandy's face hardened in a cold, bitter frown and she turned away without bothering to close the closet doors. "Maybe you'd better tell me why you're looking for that particular coat, Tom," she said sharply. "I think I have the right to know."

From the steely glint in her eyes and the razor edge in her voice, Tom knew he had struck pay dirt at last. Norman Garrison had given a fabulous fur coat to a woman all right, but not to his wife. And the woman he had given it to had worn it when she went to visit him after hours in the hospital the night he died.

Chapter Twelve

The Truth Will Set You Free

"The coat you're looking for is a chinchilla. It's one of a kind and very dramatic. It belongs to Norman's secretary, Tina Richards, and she loves to flaunt it," Sandy had said.

Her bitter words echoed in Tom's mind as he watched Tina Richards bustle into the conference room and seat herself prominently in the front row. Moments later the four judges took their places with John Dixon again sitting on the end. Tom couldn't be sure, but for an instant he thought he saw a flicker of surprise in Dixon's eyes when he saw Tina.

Getting up quickly, Tom hitched his thumbs in the vest of his three-piece suit and walked up to the conference table. "Gentlemen," he began, "we have requested this second hearing so that my father, Dr. Bob Hughes, can clear his name, once and for all. A man with a reputation and a record as impeccable as my father's should not have to prove his innocence. His years of distinguished medical service should be proof enough. Unfortunately, that is not the case at Oakdale Memorial."

The hospital administrator tried to cut in, but Tom stopped him. "Please," Tom insisted, holding up his hand. "I would like the opportunity to finish. I assure you our defense will be brief. We have just two witnesses whom you seem to have overlooked. I won't presume to cast judgment on your motives for such an oversight. When the witnesses have finished, we will allow you as much time as you require to defend your position and actions."

The two board members nodded, realizing that the hospital's good image required them to do whatever was necessary to be fair. Their agreement silenced the administrator. Of the four judges, only John Dixon betrayed no reaction. But looking closer, Tom thought he saw a tightening around the mouth, indicating that Dixon wasn't as confident as he was pretending to be.

"I think we can all agree," Tom went on, "that nothing is to be gained by repeating the charges and asking the witnesses who have already been heard to give their testimony again. Suffice it to say that the last hearing found my father, Dr. Robert Hughes, guilty of causing the death of his patient, Norman Garrison, by arguing with him and thereby triggering a fatal heart attack. The truth is that someone did argue with Garrison that night, but it wasn't my father. He arrived in the room just moments—seconds even —after Garrison's last visitor left. In fact," Tom said, allowing his voice to rise dramatically, "they brushed by each other in the hall, but my father was too preoccupied to notice who it was. In retrospect, he had a vague memory of a great fur collar pulled up high. Whose face was hidden by that luxurious collar?"

Tom paused and looked intently at each judge, allowing his gaze to focus for several seconds on the taut countenance of John Dixon. Listening to Tom and seeing Tina Richards sitting in the front row, nervously swinging her crossed leg up and down had drained the blood from his face. His hands, which he had clenched under the table, had turned clammy and a sickening feeling was growing in the pit of his stomach. He knew he had to do something quickly, or his reputation at Oakdale Memorial was going to be destroyed completely. But before he could interrupt, Tom began to speak again.

"There is a woman here who is prepared to answer that question. I don't believe I need to introduce her to most of you, but for the record, her name is Hannah Davis and she was the acting head nurse on the eleventh floor the day Norman Garrison died. Her shift was four P.M. to midnight. The rest I will leave to her to tell. Mrs. Davis." He turned and gestured to the nurse.

Smiling warmly at Tom, Hannah Davis stood up self-consciously, smoothed her skirt over her hips and, clutching her handbag tightly, walked to the front of the room.

"Now, Mrs. Davis." The administrator leaned over the table. "You don't have to tell us anything that you're not absolutely certain of. In fact, if there's any doubt in your mind, it might be wise not to say anything at all."

Hannah Davis looked at him with an unnerving directness. "I see what you mean, sir," she agreed. "But the fact is there is no doubt at all in my mind. Mr. Garrison always had the same visitor every night. And it didn't matter a bit to either of them that she always came after hours, and they were breaking hospital rules. You can ask the woman yourself. She's sitting right there in the front row big as life," Hannah said, gesturing with her head to indicate Tina Richards.

As all eyes focused on her, Tina unconsciously reached up and fluffed her platinum hair. But Hannah wasn't ready to give up the floor yet. "Now," she looked pointedly at the administrator, "if it's all the same with you, I'd like to get along with what I came here to say. The night Mr. Garrison died, I went in to check his vital signs just before I took my break at about ten. He was looking pretty good, all things considered. As I was going out, though, I bumped smack into that woman there. She was all dolled up in a fur coat that would knock your eyes out. It almost touched her ankles and had a huge shawl collar almost as big as a stole. She had it pulled up around her neck even though she was inside. But it was for the look, you know," she added, casting a knowing glance at the judges. "She was going in just when I was leaving. I was going to remind her that visiting hours were over, but I knew that I might as well save my breath. The likes of her wasn't going to listen to anybody like me."

"Mrs. Davis," the administrator interrupted, "did you also see Dr. Hughes that night?"

"Not a trace of him." She shook her head firmly. "Until I got back from my break. Then he was on the phone at the nurses' station, and he sounded very upset."

"And that was the first time you saw my father that night?" Tom asked.

"The very first." Hannah nodded vigorously.

"Thank you." Tom smiled in gratitude. "Now, unless there's any objection, I'd like to ask Ms. Tina Richards to tell you her story," he said, turning to address the judges directly.

"As a matter of fact, there is an objection,"

Dixon cut in tartly. "This whole business is a complete waste of our time. We made our decision, and we're four very busy men. I, for one, can't afford to waste my time listening to Bob Hughes's son tell us about what a great guy his father is. Can we really be expected to believe that Tom Hughes or anybody he digs up to testify is objective? If this were a court of law the whole crowd of them would be kicked out as prejudicial witnesses. Under the circumstances, I move that this hearing be adjourned permanently. There is no reason to doubt the decision we made, gentlemen."

Pushing back his chair, Dixon started to get up, but seeing that his fellow judges didn't move, he hesitated, uncertain and afraid. After a nervous glance at the two board members, the administrator decided that it was important to continue. If they appeared to be railroading Bob Hughes, it would be bad for the hospital's image.

"I think we should hear what Ms. Richards has to say, since she's taken the trouble of coming down here today. I'm sure if she agrees to be brief, you won't mind sparing us a few more minutes, Dr. Dixon."

John Dixon sank back into his seat and stared fixedly at Tina Richards who had just stood up and was beginning to walk to the front of the room. *She looks almost composed,* he thought. *Certainly much less nervous than she was the afternoon she visited my office. If she'll only stick to the story I told her.*

"Thank you for coming today, Ms. Richards," Tom began once Tina had gotten to the front of the room. "I appreciate it, and I know my father does too."

"I don't want to say anything to get myself in trouble. I told you that," she said, casting a wary look in John Dixon's direction. "If I were smart, I'd probably take the Fifth."

"There's absolutely nothing for you to worry about, I assure you," Tom said soothingly. "I'm sure the gentlemen will agree that anything you say here today will go no farther than this room."

When the judges nodded, he went on with renewed confidence. "Now, Tina, just tell us in your own words exactly what you remember about the night Norman Garrison died."

"Well, I'll try," she began hesitantly. "If you're sure it's okay. I mean, I don't want to cut my own throat, so to speak." Looking from Tom's eager face to John Dixon's taut, intense one, Tina wished she'd stayed home in bed. The young lawyer had been so convincing when he first talked to her that she'd wanted to do the right thing. But Dr. Dixon had been convincing too. She didn't know which man to believe. Tom had told her that the only possible criminal charge she faced was withholding information, if she failed to show up at the hearing. But Dr. Dixon had said the police would charge her with Norman Garrison's death if she ever admitted the truth. *It was the damn coat that got me into such a corner,* she thought miserably. *Why did I have to wear it that night?*

"Tina," Tom said coaxingly. "We're all waiting. Anytime you're ready to begin."

"Of course," she muttered, as if she'd momentarily forgotten where she was and what she was being called upon to do. "For those of you who don't know, I was a friend of Norm's—a real close friend," she added for Sandy's benefit. "I used to go to visit him every night when he was in the hospital, but like the other woman said, I went late because . . ." She faltered for a second, then quickly recovered. "Well, I guess you all know how lonesome you can get in the hospital lying there in bed hour after hour. It wasn't like Norm was much of a reader or anything like that. He was even lousy at solitaire." She glanced at Tom for approval, and when he flashed her a smile, she pushed her hair back and proceeded with renewed confidence.

"Anyway, to get to the night . . . the night Norm died. Well, it's true. I got to Norm's room just as that Davis nurse was coming out with one of those electronic thermometers in her hand. She never even said hello, not a word, but I didn't care. I went in anyway. Norm was sitting up in the bed, looking terrific like there wasn't a thing the matter with him. But he wasn't real happy to see me. I don't know what it was with him. On the outside, he could never get enough of me. But once he got sick, he didn't want to know me. Like I said to Dr. Dixon, the hospital did very strange things to Norm."

"Like you what?" Tom broke in sharply.

Tina looked up at him, surprised to be interrupted in the middle of her story. "Like I said to Dr. Dixon," she repeated blankly, "when I went to his office."

"What were you doing in John Dixon's office?" Tom fired his question like a submachine gun.

Dixon tried to intervene, to head Tina off before she said something totally damning, but he didn't have a chance. "I wanted his advice," Tina was already saying. "I heard he was interested in Norm's case and I knew he'd tell me the right thing to do. That's what doctors are for, aren't they? I was such a basket case," she admitted, shaking her head at the memory.

"And did Dr. Dixon help you?" Tom asked.

"Oh, yes," Tina responded fervently. "He was terrific. He gave me all the time in the world."

"Then maybe you'd tell us what Dr. Dixon told you to do," Tom said.

"Hold on there just a minute!" Dixon shouted, his face contorted by an expression of intense fury.

But Tina was like a musical doll. She was too wound up now to be stopped until her song ran out. "He said not to tell anybody that Norm and I had a fight that night before Dr. Hughes got there, and—"

"That's a lie!" John Dixon leaped to his feet and yelled. His face was chalk white, so were his knuckles as he clutched the edge of the table to keep himself from rushing forward and forcibly shutting Tina's mouth. "This woman is no patient of mine. I've never set eyes on her before, and I'll give you my office records to prove it," he added, knowing how easily he could doctor them to eliminate any mention of her visit.

But Tina had already opened her over-sized shoulder bag and was rummaging through it. She didn't like to be accused of lying, especially in front of so many important people. She was on the level and she intended to prove it. Doctor or not, John Dixon couldn't talk about her like that and get away with it. Triumphantly, she fished a white card out of her wallet and held it up. It was an appointment card from the office of John Dixon, M.D., giving the date and time of her visit.

Taking the card from her outstretched hand, Tom stared at it as if he didn't trust what his eyes were telling him. Then without so much as a glance at Dixon, he passed it to the hospital administrator. "I think at least three of you judges will be interested in seeing this," he said coldly. "As for the fourth, in my humble judgment, John Dixon has a lot of explaining to do. I, for one, would like him to begin right now."

Before anyone could say anything more, Dixon pushed back his chair so violently that it toppled over behind him. He knew all too well the gamble he'd taken to settle an old score with Bob Hughes. He'd gone too far, and there was no turning back. Bob Hughes would be exonerated while he, John Dixon, might be in serious trouble.

Dixon knew he could plead for leniency, but that wasn't his style. He wasn't going to crawl for any man, especially Bob Hughes. He would never give Bob or Bob's son that satisfaction. The clamor that the appointment card had caused in the room was dying down. And the administrator was turning toward him, shock written clearly on his pale face.

"Dr. Dixon," he began in a halting voice. "In light of what has been disclosed here today, I'm sure you'd like to clear up your part in this case. I know we would all . . ." He broke off in confusion.

Dixon simply turned his back on the hearing, closing the distance between the judges' table and the red neon exit sign.

"Dr. Dixon, Dr. Dixon! What do you have to say for yourself?"

The administrator's agitated cry followed

Dixon like a taunting echo as he strode out of the conference room. He'd waited years to get back at Bob Hughes, and he'd wait forever if that's what it took. But one day, he *would* get even. Bob Hughes might have won this battle, but he still had a long, dirty war ahead of him.

Chapter Thirteen
False Impressions

Sitting at the desk behind the nurses' station, John Dixon pretended to write new orders on his patients' charts. Although his head was bent as if he were concentrating entirely on the paper in front of him, he was actually listening intently to the nurses' conversation. The big news sweeping every floor of Oakdale Memorial was that Dan Stewart was back!

John's mouth hardened for a moment. The last time he'd heard that news it spelled the beginning of trouble for his marriage. He'd almost lost Kim forever. But this time he heard the news smugly. Dan Stewart was no longer a threat. He'd been sure of that since the day Kim had told him she was pregnant.

A sudden flutter of whispers and giggles caused him to look up abruptly. Dan Stewart was walking down the corridor with Bob

Hughes. A sneer spread over John's face at the sight of the two men he detested most.

John slipped unnoticed down the hall as the nurses bombarded Dan and Bob with welcoming words. He waited, biding his time until the two doctors finished thanking the women and continued down the corridor where he could corner them. One day, he vowed to himself again, he would get back at Bob Hughes, but now he was going to turn the knife in Dan Stewart. If anyone had it coming, he did, John thought remorselessly.

As the two men approached, he stepped out into their path. Ignoring Bob as though he had ceased to exist, John smiled coldly at Dan. "Long time no see."

Dan swallowed the rage that boiled up within him at the sight of John Dixon. Much as he detested the man, Dixon was Kim's husband, and he longed for her so intensely that he couldn't hold back the question that burned in his heart. "How is your wife, John?" Dan asked as evenly as he could. "I understand she's gotten over her amnesia."

"Completely." A smile of total victory curled the corners of his mouth. "Kim's memory is sharper than it's ever been, and she is blissfully happy. Finally, after all these years, she's going to have the one thing she longed for—a baby, our baby."

There was no way the two men could hide their total surprise. If Dixon had told them Kim were flying to the moon, they couldn't have been more shocked. Dumbfounded, they stared at him incredulously. Bob was the first to find his voice. It wasn't that he begrudged Kim a child. Jennifer had always said that her sister would make a wonderful mother. But he couldn't believe she had decided to have John's child after all the trouble they'd had in their marriage.

"Well, I guess congratulations are in order," he murmured. "I can't think of anyone who would be a better mother than Kim. Give her my best," he added as warmly as he could. Bob Hughes could afford to be magnanimous, even to John Dixon. Although the judges still had not delivered a second verdict in the Norman Garrison case, there was little doubt at Oakdale Memorial that Bob would be completely cleared and John was in for some pretty serious trouble. Privately, many doctors and nurses were gossiping that his days at the hospital were already numbered. But Bob wasn't one to crow over anybody else's suffering, even when it was so justly deserved.

Ignoring Bob's gracious words, John fixed Dan with a gloating look, thoroughly enjoying the other man's obvious dismay. Dan tried to swallow the lump that filled his throat. John's news had shattered his last hope. He'd pinned all his dreams on coming back from South America to Kim's love. Now he thought bitterly that he had been a fool. Kim didn't love him any more. She didn't need him. She didn't want him. How could she be having Dixon's child unless they were living together again as husband and wife?

The thought was too painful to dwell on, yet he couldn't erase it from his mind. The picture of Kim with John gnawed at his heart. He felt totally empty, drained of every emotion. Still he had to say something. Dixon was waiting.

More than anything at that moment, Dan wanted to wipe the smug expression off Dixon's face with his fist, but in the mood he was in, he knew that if he ever began to hit John, he wouldn't be able to stop until he'd beaten Dixon senseless. Normally Dan abhorred violence, but nothing short of reducing John to a bloody pulp would assuage the fury that was choking him. What had John done to turn Kim's heart so radically? How could she have changed so completely? She had loved him once. Dan was as certain of that as he was of anything in his life. He still loved her. He always would. Now, the very love that had once filled his heart felt twisted and dirtied.

He wished he'd never come back to Oakdale. He should have stayed in South America, but even that far away he'd seen Kim in every face, every window. He'd heard her voice in the peal of every bell, the trill of every exotic bird. And Betsy and Emily had been terribly homesick. There had been nothing they could recognize, nothing they could cling to until they became oriented to their new life. So, lonesome and heartsick himself, Dan had finally relented and brought his family home, only to be faced with John Dixon's devastating news.

Dan turned away, unable to bear seeing the triumphant expression on Dixon's face a second longer. "Give Kim my very best," he murmured through the unshed tears that stung his eyes. "She deserves every shred of happiness that comes to her."

Without daring to say another word or to look at John again, he turned away and headed for the elevator. He wanted to get as far away from John Dixon as he possibly could. Just seeing him and thinking of Kim in John's arms filled him with nausea. Bob Hughes was at his side offering the silent comfort of his presence. For the first time since Jennifer's death, Bob felt at peace with himself and the world. Painful though it had been, the hospital hearing had taught him an important lesson. He was not alone against the world. He had his honor, his integrity, his professional skill, and last, but very far from least, he had his children: Tom, who had grown into a source of pride and comfort, and Frannie, who remained a constant joy in his life and a fount of love. How could a man with so much not consider himself blessed?

Looking at his friend, Bob realized that for now there was nothing he could do. Dan needed to be alone. He was moving like a robot, operating entirely on automatic drive, pushing the elevator button, getting in, riding downstairs with one thought in mind: to get away from the hospital, away from John Dixon, away from Oakdale. But that was impossible now. He'd just brought the girls back. He couldn't tear them away from their home again.

Once he reached his car, Dan sank into the driver's seat and rested his head on the steering wheel. The tears that he'd been holding back stung his cheeks. The winter day when he had walked through the snow-covered woods with Kim seemed years ago. Yet, at the same time, if he shut his eyes tightly enough, he could feel her in his arms again. He could almost feel the warmth of her slender body pressed close against his and taste her lips showering him with a thousand hungry kisses.

All that was lost to him forever. All that she had given him belonged to John Dixon now. If he hadn't heard it directly from Dixon's own lips, Dan would never have believed it. Kim had never loved her husband. From the very first, theirs had been a marriage born of desperation. Through the years, John had used every trick he could think of to hold her against her will. Finally, Dan thought, he had succeeded.

A terrible sob shuddered through his rugged frame. Dan hadn't cried since Liz's death, but now he couldn't hold back any longer. His iron-tight control snapped and, clinging to the steering wheel of his car, he wept his heart out. The message from Kim seemed painfully clear. If she still loved him, she would have come to him when she had regained her memory. If she had loved him, she would never be having John Dixon's baby. Dan had dreamed that one day he and Kim would have a child, a little brother or sister for Betsy and Emily. The shattered dreams he'd held on to so tightly pounded painfully in his mind. She would never have his child now.

"Kim! Kim! How could you do it?" Dan cried. The question was wrung from the depths of his heart, rooted in love and framed in despair, but would it ever be answered now? Would Kim ever explain her change of heart? Was he doomed to live forever with the anguished question festering in his soul like an open wound?

Chapter Fourteen
Mother and Child

"Bills, bills, bills," Kim said briskly, flipping through a stack of mail. A plate of scrambled eggs sat untouched in front of her. She knew she had to eat it now that she was feeding two, but she had no appetite for food. In fact, she had no appetite for anything at all. "And here's a letter from the hospital, John. You finish your coffee," she insisted as he reached for it. "I'll read it to you."

Before he could stop her, she opened the envelope. "It's nothing important," John snapped. "Just give it to me and I'll take care of it later." He reached for it, but she shook her head and kept the letter.

"Really, John, you must have gotten up on the wrong side of the bed this morning. It's no trouble at all for me to read it," Kim assured him opening the envelope.

"Give it to me, Kim," he demanded, a tremor of desperation in his voice. "I don't want you upsetting—" Seeing her face turn as gray as the skies outside their breakfast-room window, John stopped in midsentence. "You might as well read it aloud, then," he muttered angrily.

But Kim couldn't force her lips to say the words. Instead she thrust the letter in front of him. It was exactly what he'd been afraid of, an official communique from the hospital board of directors. The verdict was finally in on the Norman Garrison case, and the judgment was unanimous. Bob was vindicated completely and given a formal apology; John, however, was to be severely punished.

Burying his face in his hands, John bit his lip to hold back the bitter emotions that flooded through him. There would be no slap on the wrist, no severe reprimand, no temporary suspension for him. The letter was terse and unequivocal. Dr. John Dixon was relieved of all duties and privileges at the hospital, effective immediately.

They fired me, he thought, *after all I've done for Oakdale Memorial Hospital.* Sinking his nails into his forehead, John tried to get a grip on himself, but his control was slipping away like quicksand. He'd played hardball and lost, but he couldn't let Kim see how much the board's action hurt him. Even though he'd been sacked unceremoniously from the hospital where he'd served for years, John wanted to stand tall in his wife's eyes.

"What does it mean, John? What have you done?"

Forcing himself to smile grimly, he looked up at her. "It means I'm never going to set foot in Oakdale Memorial, even if the entire hospital staff gets down on its collective knees and begs," he answered sharply. "And neither are you. We'll go someplace else to have the baby. No child of mine is going to be born in that place, not after today."

Kim stared at him as if she couldn't believe such a thing could happen to him. What had John done? What heinous crime had he committed? She'd been a doctor's wife long enough to know that a physician was not dismissed except for the gravest offense. In all the years they'd been married, she remembered it occurring only once before. It had been one of the worst scandals in Oakdale history. An alcoholic surgeon had been sacked after going into surgery drunk. The patient had died on the operating-room table.

"John," she gasped, "I can't believe it. This must be some awful joke. You've never even breathed a word about any trouble at the hospital, and now, out of the blue. . . ."

"Believe it, Kim," he muttered, "because it's no mistake. This letter," he said, crumbling it in his hand, "is official."

"But what's happened? What have you

done?" Kim knew she was shouting at him but she couldn't help herself.

"It's nothing you have to worry about," he snapped back. "Pregnant women shouldn't be upset."

"Shouldn't be upset?" she echoed. "How can I help being upset when my husband gets kicked out of the hospital and I'm probably the last person in Oakdale to know anything about it. I'm your wife, John," she insisted. "I have a right to know, and if you refuse to discuss this with me, then I'll find out the truth from someone else."

John laughed harshly. Before her amnesia, Kim would have turned to Dan Stewart for the sordid story, but she hadn't mentioned him since her memory had returned. "Who do you think is going to tell you?" he demanded darkly.

"My brother-in-law happens to be on the staff, too, or have you forgotten?" she retorted, instantly regretting her bold words.

At the mention of Bob Hughes, John's face turned white with rage. "I forbid you to ever speak to that guy again," he commanded in a dangerously low voice. "It's all because of him that I'm being humiliated."

Mustering a strength she didn't know she had, Kim faced him squarely. "I want you to start at the beginning, John, and tell me exactly what you did to get yourself dismissed from the hospital. If you refuse, I'm going to ask Bob, and there is no way in the world you can stop me this time."

She had a steely determination he had never seen before. For once, he realized, Kim wasn't going to allow herself to be manipulated. If he refused, she would go to Hughes, and he couldn't bear that. But if he confessed honestly and contritely, she would have to forgive him. She always had before, no matter what he'd done or how he'd tricked her, and now she was carrying his baby. They were locked together, he thought confidently, for better or worse.

But listening to John's confession, Kim felt her last small dream dissolving. It was like focusing a camera, she thought dismally. Her worst suspicions were clarifying before her eyes. John was a vicious, vindictive man. If he would frame Bob for an indiscretion committed years ago, what would he do to Dan if he ever got the chance? If he could read the secrets imprinted in her heart, measure the wealth of love that still burned inside her, feel the heat of the passion that enflamed her even now when she was pregnant with his baby?

"How could you, John?" she asked. Kim felt as if her life was being shattered, just when she'd patched the bits and pieces back together again.

John would be home now, all day, every day, Kim thought. She had imagined the happy times she and the baby would spend together, just the two of them in their own private world. It was what had made her pregnancy bearable. But that was impossible now. There would always be the three of them: the baby, herself and John. John—the wrong husband, the wrong father, the wrong lover. Although Kim knew she would love the baby no matter who the father was, she wished desperately it had been Dan's child that grew within her, Dan's loving eyes that were watching her grow. But, she told herself firmly, there was no point in dreaming. Dan Stewart was a closed chapter in her life. For a few glorious months she had lived a fantasy with him. She had opened her heart completely, holding nothing back. No thought had been too deep or too frivolous to share with him. No desire was too intimate, no dream too secret. In his strong, tender arms, in the tumultuous passion of his embrace, she'd discovered undreamed of happiness.

No matter how brief it had been or how painful the memories were now, she could never forget what once had been. The memory of every moment they had shared, every touch, every glance was indelibly imprinted on her heart. But just to survive, to go on living with the terrible pain of loss, Kim had forced herself to bury her love for Dan in the farthest recesses of her mind. The thought that Dan no longer loved her, that after she had poured out her heart to him on his telephone answering machine he had left for

South America without a word had crushed her spirit completely.

When she realized that Dan was lost to her, Kim had made up her mind to stay with John, to keep their family together for the unborn child's sake. Now, though, she knew she couldn't go through with her plan. Gradually, through the years of their marriage, she had come to realize that her husband was a cynical, twisted man. But until now, she had never realized how vicious he could be. Too profoundly shocked to forgive and forget yet another time, she knew that it was impossible to go on living with him even a day longer. How could she expect their baby to grow up healthy and happy with a father such as John?

Even as she faced him across the breakfast table, her clear, honest eyes filled with naked disgust, Kim didn't doubt that he loved her in his peculiar, twisted way.

"Everything I did or tried to do to Bob Hughes, I did for you, because of the way he treated you," John was insisting. "All these years I've loathed him. Every day that I met him in the hospital, I vowed to myself that as soon as I saw my chance I would get even with him for making you pregnant, then abandoning you like the coward he is. How can you hate me for that, darling?"

"That's not love, John," she retorted, an intense feeling of loathing welling up inside her. "That's a sickness, and I can't live with it any longer. I know what you've done. I know how you've tried to use my amnesia to hold on to me, to make me a virtual slave of your love. But I remember everything now, John. *Everything.* Before the tornado, I asked you for a divorce and you agreed. Now, I'm not asking. I'm demanding one."

For a long moment, John stared at her blankly, as if no emotion, no disaster or triumph could ever move him again. This time he knew he had finally and totally lost. He could still deny Kim a divorce, but it would be an empty victory. With or without one, she was walking out of his life forever.

Tears formed in his pale eyes making them glisten. "I'll change, Kim," he begged, but she was already shaking her head. He knew suddenly that it was no use to fight anymore, no use to argue, no use to get down on his knees. Dropping his napkin on his plate, he stood up.

"Whatever you want, Kim . . . darling, Kim," he added, knowing that he was saying it for the very last time. He left the room, not wanting to break down in front of her.

The scrambled eggs sat growing cold on her plate, but Kim had forgotten about the wasted breakfast. She was thinking ahead to the life she faced now. She'd be a single parent with an infant baby and a broken heart to nurse. For a blissful moment she allowed herself to dream. If only Dan would come back to Oakdale . . . back to her.

But would he want her now? Would he be able to accept John's baby even if he still loved her? Clasping her hands protectively over her belly, Kim whispered to her baby, "Like it or not, all we've got now is each other. It's you and me against the world."